A Spellster N

SOMEONE ELSE'S SHOES

ALDREA ALIEN

Thardrandian Publications

For information contact:
http://www.aldreaalien.com

Cover design by Aldrea Alien

ISBN: 978-0-9922645-9-8
First Edition: November 2021

10 9 8 7 6 5 4 3 2 1

Dedicated to my
critique partners, my editor, beta
and sensitivity readers.

Chapter 1

"You missed a spot."

Alla's humming died in her throat. Had someone spoken? To *her*? Blinking out of her trance-like daze, she lifted her attention from the marble tiles she had almost finished polishing. All around, the foyer floor glistened with her efforts.

Fingers, glittering with silver and jewels, clicked in front of Alla's face. "Did you hear me?" Tamara demanded, continuing to snap her fingers even though they were almost nose to nose. "Answer me when I speak, girl."

"I heard you," Alla retorted, cupping her ears. The dead could likely hear her stepsister, what with how abysmally loud each one of Tamara's snaps was. "It would help if you pointed out where." She spied no flaw in her work, not even when she sat back on her heels and gave each tile a critical eye.

Still, perhaps her stepsister saw something Alla couldn't.

Tamara narrowed her dark eyes. They gleamed in the midday light. Not as sharply as Alla's stepmother, but with an echo of the same cruelness she reserved for those she considered beneath her. "Right here." With a deft kick to the nearby bucket, Tamara upended the contents.

Cold, silty water splashed Alla and washed out onto the tiles.

Even knowing it was too late, Alla scrambled to her feet. The water had drenched her from top to bottom. Her hair was sodden. The skirts of her dress clung to her legs like seaweed. "What—?"

"Oh dear," Tamara gasped, poorly concealing her smirk behind her fingers. "Just look at the mess you've made, Little Soot. How clumsy of you. One would think, what with your muddled background, that you would be at least reasonably graceful."

Alla bit her tongue. Being elven—or even half—was not a guarantee of grace.

She towered over Alla. Even with them both standing upright, her stepsister was taller by at least a foot. "Looks like you're going to be here all day. What will mother say?" Giving a tweak to the tip of Alla's ear, Tamara sauntered deeper into the mansion.

Alla rubbed at her ear as she watched her stepsister depart. How she loathed the distinct points and sensitivity. What use did such ears give their owners beyond a means to single out elves as a target? Better hearing? It hardly seemed worth the trouble.

With the tips of her ears still smarting, Alla sank back to her knees and set to work mopping up the water. The cloth she had been polishing the tiles with was already sopping wet and not terribly absorbent, but its sheer size meant she could wring out a decent cupful with each pass. She would need to start her work over once this outbreak was contained. Otherwise, her stepmother would complain about how the unaffected tiles weren't as shiny.

Had she the use of her magic, she could've done the work in a quarter of the time. *And dry myself off.* But any thoughts of using her blood-born spellster abilities had been nipped in the bud by her stepmother after the first instance of Alla lighting a fire in the hearth. Even the teeniest flame, no matter the control Alla displayed over it, had been too much for her stepmother.

Alla's abilities had been neatly locked away for over a decade, kept contained by a chain necklace of purple metal no thicker than her thumb. *For my own good.* At least, that had been the excuse her stepmother had given when Alla was young. They weren't afraid of magic—they were spellsters themselves—but letting *her* have free access? Unthinkable.

Perhaps they were afraid of her inexperience. Certain magics came instinctually, but controlling them took time.

2

Something she had barely begun to manage during the time of her mother's death. Her father had stressed patience when it came to such matters. Her stepmother had thought otherwise.

Even back when the chain first graced Alla's neck, it hadn't been lost on her that some of the newly bought people her stepmother added to the household staff wore collars made of the same metal. Especially amongst those who worked the fields.

She had tried numerous times throughout her teen years to remove the impediment before concluding it just wasn't possible. Not of her own will. The chain consisted of naught but continuous loops, each one too thick to break naturally, with no actual clasp to be had. There were tools in the shed that could've aided her freedom, but using any great deal of force also risked the metal exploding.

"Oh, my lady."

Alla glanced up at the familiar cry. Her heart thumped a few extra beats as she hastened to confirm no one else but herself shared the foyer with the old woman. " 'Dett, we've spoken about this. You can't call me that. It's just Alla." No matter how many times Alla told the woman, she always had to remind Odette not to refer to her in such a manner. Neither of them could ever be too certain of some word getting back to Alla's stepmother. And if it did...?

Odette waved the concern away as if angering Alla's stepmother didn't mean a lashing. Unlike the majority of the serfs living in the estate, she had been inherited by Alla's father, much to his disapproval. But her ownership had come from well before his birth. The woman's collar still bore the family crest etched into the steel plating riveted to the old leather even though the practice of marking serfs was outdated.

There hadn't been many left in their indentured servitude before Alla's father died fighting in the imperial army. Only two such people remained now.

He had always insisted on owning no being, elven or otherwise. Alla had a great many memories of him pacing before the fireplace, furiously muttering of how many nobles leant on the same pathetic excuse of an entirely too complicated emancipation process, of how the glass barons

3

should be vilified as the abusive factories they were.

Even back then, she had known such views were considered outlandish for any noble in the Niholian Empire.

But once the news of his demise reached them, her stepmother had wasted little time in firing the free servants and trading the few able-bodied serfs for whatever took her fancy. Odette and Uda where the only two who remembered Alla's father, and they were only here because not even the glass barons wanted them.

"My dear, sweet child." Odette knelt before Alla. "Look at you. As wet as a squid and paddling about like a duck." She gently wrapped her long fingers—an elven trait Alla was relieved to have missed inheriting from her mother—around Alla's wrists. "Let's get you cleaned up and—"

"I'm fine." Alla jerked her chin at the floor. Without her trying to contain the damage, poor as her attempt had been, the water continued to spread. More seemed to have splashed from the bucket than it could possibly contain.

"Nonsense, my lady." Odette gently coaxed Alla to her feet. "You've the countess to attend to soon and you can't go to her looking like a used mop. Go clean yourself up. I'll finish here."

Alla took a step, then paused.

"Don't worry about me. I've been cleaning these floors since before you were born." She made soft shooing motions, as though Alla was still a child, before adjusting the scarf wrapped around her hair and kneeling on the tiles with a grunt.

Knowing better than to argue with the woman, Alla aimed for the hallway entrance. If she hurried, she could throw on some dry clothes and still make it in time to serve lunch.

Her stomach grumbled at the thought of food. She hadn't eaten since before sunrise but, once her stepmother and stepsister had eaten their fill, there was generally plenty to pick off their plates.

Icy water dripped on her bare feet as she took a few shuffling steps.

Her things were kept in the attic. Getting there would see her leaving a trail of water droplets all through the mansion. If her stepmother caught sight of a single one, she would see Alla received a good five lashes, the typical response to anything she perceived as a single slight.

But Alla knew of another way up the mansion, one that her stepmother wasn't likely to notice her using at this hour. It was the reason she always left the window to the attic open a crack.

She stepped outside to where a great date palm tree grew in the centre of the otherwise paved courtyard. Ferns huddled around the base, their leaves having gone brown in the summer heat. Alla squeezed all the water she could from her skirts. The droplets barely hit the parched earth before vanishing. There was nothing she could do about her hair but tie the curls back with a scarf and let it dry naturally whilst working on her afternoon duties.

The midday air, with its north-eastern breeze coming fresh off the desert, would help towards drying the threadbare fabric on her way up the mansion. It wouldn't make the dress suitable to wear by the time she reached the attic, but spreading it out on the rooftop would see it usable by tomorrow.

Alla hastened around the side of the mansion to where a stone tub full of water sat near the back door. Hopping onto the tub's rim, she scampered her way up the wall as nimbly as a mountain goat.

The path she took wasn't a well-worn one—she tried her best to not abuse this knowledge lest she got caught—but she had taken this route so many times over the years that she hardly needed to think on her next move. Her fingers just knew where they needed to be—a hand tucked into a hole in the stonework here, a foot placed on the thin ledge of a window there. As long as she didn't stop or slow for any reason, she always made it.

Up here, the farmland seemed to stretch on into the hazy, yellow horizon of the nearby desert. To her left lay the shaded pasture where the camels spent their nights. It used to house her stepmother's horses, but they had long since gone from this world. As many beings seemed to do around here.

The pasture was currently empty, the camels out in the field with the serfs who tended to the rows upon rows of crops. To some, the fields seemed endless, but Alla remembered there being so much more.

The estate had once been prosperous, home of the finest and sweetest dates in all of the Niholian Empire. She had vague memories of men and women scampering up the huge trees during harvest time to lower massive sacks of dates onto the carts. The world had smelt wet and earthy.

Now, that same dusty land didn't quite produce enough to feed those living here. Without proper care to the irrigation systems that had kept this land rich for generations, the trees had died. Only the one in the courtyard remained and even that was a sickly shadow of itself.

The attic window popped open at the slightest tug, swinging out into nothing. With one final glance at the ground to confirm no one was about, Alla squeezed herself in through to the attic. The floorboards—the years having turned the ironwood the same dark brown colour as her feet—greeted her arrival with the faintest of creaks.

So many things had been moved here over the years that an antique shop would've had a harder time looking so complete. The only thing lacking was a bed, but Alla was small enough to make do with a few cushions and an old horse rug Odette had smuggled up.

She swiftly shed her damp clothes, draping them just outside the window and pinning them down with a few strategic pieces from a broken statue of the many-armed goddess, Ara. Alla muttered a prayer to the rain goddess as she did so. Everything seemed to have gone wrong since its hectic removal from the foyer all those years ago—her mother's death, her father leaving to join the military, the estate falling into ruin.

Donning another dress, she hastened to fasten the front. Her fingers fumbled with the tiny buttons. *Come on.* Why were there so many? She disliked the dress for that very reason. "You're going to make me late," she whispered to the fabric as if it would help. If she'd but another dress to choose from...

You've more choice than most. Her stepmother's words danced through her mind.

There was a measure of truth in them. The majority of her clothes had belonged to her mother. Few were suitable for drudgery, though. Most still required her to let them out as Alla's more human-like figure had grown beyond the naturally lean one of most elves. At least the skirts hung at a modest height.

Beyond her short stature and the pointed tips to her ears, she had inherited little of her mother's elven nature. There was a great deal more about her that seemed a little too human-like. She hadn't the elongated canines, her voice couldn't trill. Any attempts to sing came out as such dreadful squawks that she hadn't tried since her childhood—and her fingers were an inch shorter than the normal length of elven digits. She possessed the heightened senses of sight and hearing, but they weren't as obvious.

So long as she kept her ears covered and her head down, she could pass as a full-blooded human, which meant she was treated more-or-less like any other human servant outside the mansion gates. Not an easy task around her stepsisters, who had made goading her into their little game.

There. Buttons finally done, Alla hastened through the hatch and out into the hall. Lunch would've been sent up from the kitchen by now. Her stepmother was going to be furious at Alla's tardiness. Neither fact could be helped, but she didn't need to compound things by lingering.

Chapter 2

It wasn't as if her stepmother—or stepsisters, when it came down to it—needed Alla to do everything for them. Those in the kitchen would have seen to the preparation of lunch and the food was no doubt waiting for someone to collect from the little serving lift in the dining room. It merely needed setting out.

That was Alla's job. Thrice a day, every day. She was expected to pour their tea and kofe, to butter their bread, to do everything but cut their food and eat it. Never mind that all it would take for the trio to eat without her merely required one of them to retrieve the tray.

The dining room was quite large and kept immaculate even though it saw no more than Alla's passage these days. The stone walls were carved with a relief of the farmland as it had once stood, with rows upon rows of date palms. Those wide, ivory-coloured leaves stretched to the ceiling where she'd a hazy memory of a glittering mosaic. The small, jewel-like tiles had gone years ago, chipped off at her stepmother's insistence on redecorating.

They had just removed the last of the tiles when the news of her father's demise reached their door.

Time had remained still for this room ever since. Her stepmother treated the dining room as if stepping into it meant certain death—even as she swore avoiding it was merely her having a preference for the intimate setting of her study—and her daughters followed suit. Alla couldn't fathom why. It wasn't a cursed place.

Sliding the latch to the serving lift open, Alla retrieved the two trays of food and made her way through the mansion. Learning to balance the trays in her hands had taken a fair bit of practice as a child, and a lot of dropped items, but she now navigated the short distance between dining room and study without a wobble.

The room's broad windows faced the west, set to catch the setting sun. Her father had preferred the library for his work, so this place had been turned into one of relaxation. The space was stuffed with an abundance of cushions and couches to lounge upon in the afternoon sun. An act her stepsisters were especially fond of and were currently doing.

It was one of the few rooms redecorated to her stepmother's tastes, the warm wood panelling painted over in a dirty cream colour and gauzy curtains draped across the tops of the windows to filter the light. The picture of her father still hung beside the fireplace. There used to be one of her mother beside it, removed when her stepmother had entered the house. A mirror sat in its place, its silvered surface cold and glinting in the light.

A gilded table with three matching chairs dominated the centre of the room. It was this that Alla aimed for.

Her stepmother stood before the mirror, one hand pressed to her jawline as she examined her reflection. She idly drummed her fingers on the mantelpiece. Unlike her stepmother's eldest daughter, Tamara, her olive-brown fingers were bare of any adornments.

That emotionless gaze flicked ever so briefly in Alla's direction. "You are late."

"Apologies, Mistress," she murmured. So many times those words had passed her lips, they'd almost become second nature when dealing with her stepmother. Ducking her head, she scuttled across the room to set the trays atop the table and busy herself with serving their food. "I got a little behind on this morning's chores and—"

Alerted to nearing footfalls at her back, Alla held her tongue. She glanced across the room at the window, the pane taking up the larger percentage of the wall, and spied the reflection of her stepmother coming towards her.

"Not terribly much," Alla amended. "Just an issue with the bucket that—"

"*Why*," her stepmother interrupted, "is your hair wet?" She stood directly behind Alla. Although the coolness of her voice was like a droplet of water down the back, her loud breathing steamed Alla's skin.

"Perhaps she was attempting to clean the ash smudges from her face," Natalya suggested before Alla could reply. Lounging upon one of the couches, she flapped her palm frond fan above her. The breeze barely disturbed the wispy pieces of her hair, the loose coils almost as light a brown as Alla's. "I don't know anyone who gets as utterly filthy just being near a fireplace as you do, Soot."

Alla reflexively rubbed her cheek against her shoulder. Her nights reading in the kitchen by the embers' meagre light and the occasional nap there in the cooler months did tend to leave her a little grubby in the morning. But she was always awake and clean before either of her stepsisters stirred for their breakfast. "No, I—"

"Maybe she went for a swim," Tamara chipped in from her place ensconced in a padded chair before the small bookcase. She glanced up from her book to smirk in Alla's direction before returning to the pages.

Alla held her tongue and busied herself with buttering a slice of bread, setting it aside to grab another slice.

"What?" Natalya gasped, sitting upright on the couch. "Not in our little lake? With all those filthy birds?" She shuddered and ran her hands down her front as if the ducks had personally defecated over her. "I thought elves drowned when you dunked them in anything deeper than a puddle."

Ruthlessly biting her tongue, Alla continued her task. Retaliation, even a verbal correction of facts, got her nothing but lashings. Ignoring her stepsisters' attempts to get a rise out of her was her only concession. Her stepmother didn't care what her daughters did, providing they didn't hamper their paltry flow of income.

Tormenting Alla didn't fall into that category.

"Tammy, dear," her stepmother said. "Do wipe that insufferable expression off your face. It's unbecoming of a lady." She settled into her usual seat and waited for Alla to load the food onto her plate. "You two really should be more mindful of your words. After all, you shall both need to present your best at the ball."

Alla paused in pouring the woman's tea. "A ball? Here?" It had been years since the mansion had seen more than the occasional wooing visitor.

"Don't be ridiculous," her stepmother snapped. "Where would we host one? Out in the courtyard like vagrants? No." She leant forward, ensuring she held Alla's attention. "At the palace." She spoke slowly, each word loud and drawn out as if Alla was some hard of hearing foreigner. "Honestly," her stepmother muttered as she sat back and picked up her teacup. "I think all that ash and soot you waddle in is affecting your brain."

"Prince Viktor will be there." Tamara sighed. "He's so handsome." She set aside her book and waved a hand at Alla, beckoning her to come closer with her kofe.

Alla hastened over with the second tray and laid out the various paraphernalia required to brew the drink. She poked the coals in the tiny brazier back to life and set the steel cup on top, angling the long handle away from her lest her stepsister chose to upend the hot kofe all over Alla. She poured the drink into the cup and returned to serving the food.

"I've always found him to be more adorable than handsome," Natalya gabbled, popping a grape into her mouth before resuming her recline in the sun. "And tidy, too. They say he's always immaculately shaven. He must do it twice a day. Do you not think so, Mother?"

Alla's stepmother hummed as she lifted the teacup to her lips. A faint grimace warped her features and the cup was lowered a mite bit faster. "The tea is cold again."

"Apologies, Mistress." She set the porcelain cup next to the brazier and tipped the foam floating on top of the not-quite-bubbling kofe into it before returning the steel cup to the glowing coals. It was almost ready to serve. Her nose told her just a few more seconds. "I will take it back once I've—"

"Now." Her stepmother rarely raised her voice. Rather, the tone shifted from mildly disgusted to hard and curt. It brought to mind images of whips and set Alla's back to tingling.

Alla hastened from the brazier, scooping the teapot from the table. "Yes, Mistress. I'll have a fresh pot sent up right away." Holding the belly of the porcelain to her chest, she scuttled for the dining room.

"Don't come back until you have," her stepmother said, the command chasing Alla as she slipped through the door.

"Foolish, girl," Alla muttered to herself once out of hearing range. Unlike the kofe beans, tea was a product of the neighbouring Udynea Empire. *And expensive.* Woefully so. Her stepmother would find a suitable punishment for wasting an entire pot, never mind that anything not consumed by the trio was generally gnawed upon by the kitchen staff. The woman still considered it as wasteful as if Alla had poured it onto the ground.

But who would she blame this time? The cook? One of the kitchen staff? Alla?

Her back itched at the thought. She could handle another lashing. It had been a week since the last one—courtesy of Natalya's magic and over a stocking the woman had misplaced—plenty of time for her body to heal. Another gift from her elven bloodline.

The slap of her bare feet on the floorboards was the only sound as she crossed the dining room.

Setting the teapot into the lift, she pulled out a scrap of paper from her dress pocket and scribbled a quick explanation for its swift return. Not words. Beyond the head cook, the kitchen was manned by serfs. Whilst a few of the upper servants, such as the cook, understood the written word, the rest hadn't been given the opportunity to read.

In her effort to negate the need for every one of her stepmother's requests to be run by one person, Alla had taught those in the kitchen a series of symbols. Not words, per se, but simpler.

Message written, she released the lever holding the lift in place and slowly tugged on the rope. The lift lowered in increments, jerking and rattling all the way. Once, it had been a smooth-running contraption that barely announced its arrival. Age and the lack of grease had snatched away all the effortless grace.

The serving lift only travelled down from here, not merely to the kitchen a floor below, but further still to the cellar. She recalled many a time in her childhood of squeezing herself into the box. Even if she wasn't a touch bit too big to fit now, she wouldn't risk her life to the thing.

The rope on her hands jerked. She pulled a little harder and was met with resistance. The lift had arrived. Nothing to do but wait for its return.

Leaning back on the wall, Alla slid down until her backside hit the floor. A reprieve from chores during the day was rare.

Her thoughts drifted. *A ball.* She had been too young for the last one. Her mother had gone, the presence of an elf on a count's arm surprising everyone and making him something of a pariah to all but the royal family. Alla still recalled her mother's description of the palace and its seemingly endless garden with its exotic plants that shouldn't survive under the Niholian sun but still prospered.

It all sounded like a dream.

Alla closed her eyes as she imagined actually entering the palace gates and seeing the magnificence of the ballroom, of stepping into the flourishing gardens. She had seen the outside of the palace, albeit from a distance whilst buying food at the market. The pale building loomed over the city, its shimmering domes a beacon to all who trod the roads leading to the capital.

She hadn't ever seen the gates, never mind beyond them. But she could imagine the gardens bright and green like the mansion flowerbeds from her childhood. There'd be the crisp scent of the earth and the perfume of a dozen different buds all mingling on the sea air. The grass would be springy beneath her feet and the trees would shade great swathes of the garden, just begging for someone to lie beneath their boughs. And the—

The rattle of the lift jerked Alla back into the dining room.

She scrambled to her feet as the teapot rose into sight. Barely waiting for the lift to click into its holding position, she claimed the tray and scuttled back into the study to pour her stepmother a fresh cup. The fresh pot was met with a cool, silent nod as the woman drank.

Tamara cleared her throat. "My kofe?" She waved a hand at the metal cup still balanced above the brazier.

Alla's stomach sank. Had the woman really left it brewing this whole time? Could it be salvaged? Perhaps if she sweetened it enough, it would mask the bitterness.

Steeling herself, she marched over to pour her stepsister's kofe. All it needed was transferring to the cup already full of foam, an act she knew Tamara could do herself.

Only after Alla had drizzled a liberal amount of honey in with the mixture did she hand over the cup.

Her stepsister inhaled deeply before taking a sip. "It's over-brewed, cold and *sweet*." She gagged as if Alla had tried to poison her. "Don't you know how to make decent kofe by now?"

"Apologies." Alla scooped up the cup in both hands. A faint warmth radiated from the porcelain. "I'll—"

"Stay right where you are, girl. For heaven's sake, Tammy, dear, no one ever died from drinking cold kofe. I don't know how you manage to consume such hot liquids on a day like this." She picked up her teacup and took a savouring sip. Her gaze fastened on Alla with all the welcome of a branding poker. "Tammy was telling me she found one of the serfs cleaning the foyer floor this morning. That's one of your jobs, is it not?"

"Yes, stepmother." She glanced at Tamara, who smirked around her cup, then returned her focus to the woman's mother. "The bucket was knocked over and I got soaked. Odette offered to clean up whilst I changed."

"And, consequently, she was late for her duties."

"Punished most brutally for it, too," Natalya murmured, the first she'd spoken since Alla had re-entered the room. She waved for the tray of food to be brought closer.

Alla obliged the request even as her grip tightened on the tray and visions of smashing her stepsister's head with the underside danced through her mind. Of the three, only Natalya seemed to take pleasure in punishing those she saw as beneath her.

With great control, she managed to stay her hands and let her stepsister pluck a fresh handful of grapes from the bowl. Natalya gave her fan a few flaps, further disturbing the warm air but doing little else.

"Unfortunate," her stepmother replied with a crisp shake of her head. She tore a mouthful of bread from a slice, grimacing as she chewed. "This bread is gritty. What is our miller doing with it these days?"

"Our mill hasn't ground flour for years, Mistress." The windmill's sails had been taken down after a young man, one of those her stepmother bought, had gotten his legs accidentally crushed beneath the millstone.

Her stepmother's eyes widened, the stare blank for a breath before focusing on Alla. "I know that." She slammed the slice onto the plate. "If this is the best you can get at the market, then maybe I need to send someone else."

"Not at all," Alla insisted. Her journey to buy from the market what they couldn't produce was the highlight of her month. That time was swiftly approaching. *Two days.* She would leave at dawn, drive the cart into the capital, arrive at the market square at midday and return home before the afternoon was done with the world. All the while being utterly alone, except for the occasional companionship of Odette or Uda.

"Don't forget my order," Tamara said. "And check them. The last basket of figs you bought were half-rotten."

"*Our* orders," Natalya sharply amended, glaring at her sister.

"Of course, dear sisters. I would never forget either of you." She'd a rather vivid memory—and the hint of a scar on her right arm—that ensured she didn't overlook even the smallest of their requests.

Content that her services wouldn't be requested immediately, Alla stepped back against the wall to wait whilst the trio consumed their lunch. When they'd eaten their fill, she carried the trays back to the lift and lowered them to the kitchen before returning to clean the study.

Chapter 3

A basket of figs for Tamara, another of grapes for Natalya. Alla ticked the items off her mental list as the merchants' servants loaded the wares onto her cart before she urged the camels on to the next stall. Her stop at the vegetable section of the square to collect squash seeds, to grow before the coming winter, had been brief. That left her with one thing to procure. *Ten sacks of flour.*

As always, an irate niggle furrowed her brow. They had once grown all the food they could ever require on the estate. Unlike the dates, it was never in amounts that made it profitable to sell, but enough that supplementation hadn't been necessary. But the fig trees had died in the last drought and the grapevines put out barely enough to make raisins.

Still, the lack of such home-grown produce gave her an excuse to be in the city market. The freedom of leaving the estate, the crisp air on the drive down, the thrill of guiding the camels through the roads. It didn't matter the trip was only once a month. She even loved haggling with the merchants, who treated her as an equal.

Unless they happened to spot her ears.

She kept them covered with curls of hair pinned neatly in place. Not everyone treated elven people with disdain, but enough did to make revealing her true self to strangers a gamble. It was one she wasn't prepared to bet her life on.

If only she wasn't travelling alone. But Uda had her own duties to attend and Odette wasn't able to climb onto the cart, not without aggravating the lash welts on her back. Even after the better part of two days, they weren't healing as swiftly as they used to.

Alla wished she had enough money left over to get a proper healing balm rather than relying on the poultices the cook whipped together.

Except there would be nothing after purchasing the flour needed for daily bread to feed everyone at the estate. Her stepmother made sure of that. The woman counted every penny before Alla left and, even though the price of goods fluctuated throughout the year, she expected Alla to return with the same amount regardless of circumstances.

It certainly wasn't the countess and her daughters who went without during the leaner times. If she was as stringent on their spending, they could've afforded far more than gritty flour and barely edible fruit. Nevertheless, Alla did her best to adhere to her stepmother's wishes.

Today, it seemed that goal wasn't going to be so easily accomplished. Otherwise, she would be on her way home with her haul rather than still haggling with the miller in the noon sun over a few pennies.

"I understand what you're asking for, my lady," the man said. "But I simply cannot accept so little for ten sacks."

The courtesy the miller gave her was due to her consistent custom, a loyalty that went back as far as her father, but the title was thanks to her garb. The threadbare silk of her skirts once bore silver embroidery and tiny, multi-coloured glass beads. All of it picked clean when Natalya had grown weary of the outfit and magnanimously gifted it to Alla. It was a little on the cumbersome side and dull without its embellishments.

Still, pretty gowns wouldn't sway the miller on his prices. If anything, it could work against her. Only noblewomen and wealthy merchants dared to walk the streets garbed thusly. "You accepted that amount last month," she reminded him. "And in the months before."

"But that was then. With the cost of water these days..." He scratched at his whiskered cheek. The sight of facial hair was always an odd one for Alla, no matter how often she saw it, and made her face itch just looking at it. Elves couldn't grow beards and her father had preferred to remain clean-shaven.

"Factoring in how the crops have been fairing..."

"Which is exceptionally well. Or so my sources tell me." Of course, those sources were her own ears as she rode through the city, but she wasn't about to tell him that. "And you agreed on keeping it at that price for this month when we last spoke." It wouldn't matter if the man hadn't. Her offer was all the money she had left.

The miller grunted. He rubbed at his ruddy nose, sniffing pitifully even as the act disturbed flakes of skin. "You'll beggar an old man over a sack of flour?"

Alla laughed. "I hardly think paying a penny's difference a sack will beggar you, Master Miller." She leant closer. "And I know you're diluting it with stone sweepings. The last lot was exceptionally gritty. If the authorities ever learnt of *that*..." She trailed off, letting her gaze drift to the guards wandering the square.

The miller scoffed. "Surely a lady of your high breeding wouldn't stoop to blackmail."

Acknowledging him with the barest of glances, Alla returned to wordlessly scrutinise the guards. There seemed to be more than usual. A few looked to be decked in the armour of those who generally guarded the palace gates.

It was the crown who decreed a certain level of quality in what was a staple for the majority of its citizens. If she alerted any of the guards to the miller's actions, they would see him fined and slapped in the stocks.

The longer Alla remained silent, the more the miller nervously shuffled on the spot and tapped his fingers on the knuckle of his opposite hand.

Finally, he wet his lips. "Ten sacks was it, then, my lady?"

"*Without* the stone sweepings?"

The man hung his head, shaking it as he sighed. "You're a hard one, girl." Turning to his workers, he ordered her cart loaded with the sacks.

Alla stepped back as she waited for them to finish. If she had the camels pick up pace once they were on the road home, she might have enough time to change into her regular clothes before serving her stepmother and stepsisters their dinner.

The whisper of the crowd grew. People bustled at Alla's back, caught up in something happening near the centre of the square. Curious, she clambered into the driver's seat to see over them.

A man dressed in the fine silken vest and trousers of a royal crier stood upon the dry fountain in the middle of the square. He held a large scroll before him. "Citizens of Niholia!" he bellowed, barely lifting his gaze from the words.

Unlike full-blooded humans, Alla heard well enough without having to press so close like the gathering crowd. Nevertheless, she took a few steps towards the man, balancing herself on the edge of the cart.

"His imperial majesty, Tsar Petya, is set to hold a ball in a week's time in honour of the Prin—"

Alla settled back into the seat and returned her attention to the man loading the sacks. What the crier said wasn't anything she hadn't heard before. A few others in the crowd must've been likewise informed, as they returned to their tasks rather than stand around as the crier continued.

"All done, my lady," said the miller loudly enough to ensure everyone heard. "Ten sacks, just as requested." He leant against the cart, peering up at her. "I trust our previous conversation will stay between us?"

Bowing her head, Alla handed over the coin. "Of course, Master Miller." As much as she didn't want to rely on something as underhanded as blackmail, no one else would sell her that much flour for such a low price. She had bellies that needed filling.

The miller stepped back, allowing Alla to urge the camels onwards. With the crowd still lingering even though the royal crier had finished, she was forced to manoeuvre the cart out of the square in a winding loop. It took her past several stalls wedged at the entrance of an alleyway.

Something small and fast caught Alla's attention like a persistent fly buzzing on the edge of her vision. She turned her head, the reins twitching in the command to halt as she tore her concentration from guiding the camels through the crowd.

A child burst from the alleyway, barrelling through the stalls, dodging the merchants crammed in there and leaping neatly over piles of wares. Throughout it all, the child kept glancing over their shoulder.

Alla jerked on the reins at the same time the child stopped

in front of her cart. The little body collided with the camels, bouncing back with a shriek.

"Goodness!" Alla leapt from the driver's seat before the cart finished coming to a halt. She rushed to the child's side. "Are you hurt?"

The girl cringed, her honey-coloured eyes wide and fearful. She was an elf, slighter than most and looked to be no more than seven years of age. Tears rolled down her grubby face in the biggest droplets Alla had ever seen. She favoured her left arm, her long fingers clutching the wrist of her other hand to her chest, but Alla couldn't be certain if the injury was recent. Or even as a result of the collision.

"It's all right," Alla said, kneeling beside the girl. "You're safe. I won't hurt you." She glanced around, searching for anyone who showed too much interest in the accident. Most of the onlookers had returned to their own tasks. Those who milled about did little more than shoot the odd disgusted glance their way—likely for the audacity of the girl causing a ruckus.

Whatever the girl had been fleeing from in the alleyway hadn't made itself known.

The girl eyed Alla with fear. Her gaze would occasionally dart towards the alleyway entrance, but her focus rested largely on Alla.

"No," Alla breathed. "Look." Carefully, she lifted her hair far enough from her ear to show the girl the point. "I'm just like you."

Disbelief narrowed the girl's eyes, but it was better than stark terror.

"Are you hurt?" Alla reached for the girl's arm, stopping when the girl jerked back. *That would be a yes, then.* It didn't look terribly bad. No swelling or discolouring to the coppery skin beyond the usual grime of street life. "Well, you can't stay in the middle of the road. Let me help you up." Taking the girl's hand, Alla gently assisted her to her feet. "Were you running from someone?"

The girl nodded, hunching her shoulders. She clutched her neck, where the grime wasn't as thick. Had she been wearing a sling? Or maybe a collar? Was she a serf? A slave? That could cause problems, especially if she was running from her owner.

Or worse, the enslavers.

"I don't suppose you have parents?" Alla asked the girl, not holding out much hope for a positive answer. "And that they're around?"

The girl shook her head.

Of course not. Sighing, she idly scratched at her wrist. What was she going to do? With the cart blocking a thoroughfare, she obviously couldn't linger to ensure the girl's safety. But if the girl kept running around the square like this, someone was going to run her over. Or worse, snaffle her up and sell her.

She *could* take the girl back to the estate. Except if her stepmother found out... The sudden appearance of another mouth would not be welcome, especially when that mouth was attached to a figure that didn't look as though they could work for long without keeling over.

She could try hiding the girl. But how?

Unlike her father, her stepmother didn't permit children to remain on the estate, trading away even the most skilful of serfs if she discovered they were pregnant, which meant Alla couldn't hide the girl amongst others her age.

Perhaps if she kept the girl in the kitchen, she could build up her endurance to work in the scullery and, by the time her stepmother found out there was another mouth on the property, the girl would be too useful to bother with her removal.

"There she is!"

Alla whirled at the cry, faint though it had been, instinctively tucking the girl behind her. *Enslavers.*

She quite clearly recalled the stories her stepmother had joyously regaled her during the first few months after her father's death. Of how urchins were a common target for enslavers and seen as a pest to those within the city. Controlling their numbers often meant rounding them up and selling them cheap to the glass barons.

Her stepmother had threatened the idea of dumping her into one such muster before apparently deciding Alla had some use around the mansion.

She hadn't expected the two men—both human, judging by the sheer broadness of their size—to look so ordinary. They marched up the same alleyway, leaning slightly towards the other as they talked naturally as any person. Except she knew what their conversation was truly about.

Unlike the nimbleness of the girl vaulting over the stalls, the enslavers would be hampered by them. There was still time.

"Climb up," Alla commanded the girl, jerking her head to indicate the cart. "I won't lie and say you'll be free of worry, but I think we both know what they have in mind for you will be worse."

The girl bit her lip and glanced uncertainly at the cart.

"My lady," someone called out. A figure to her left, brightly garbed in comparison to the dull outfits of the enslavers, hastened in her direction. "I must insist on you moving along."

Alla didn't dare turn to acknowledge them and lose focus on the enslavers' actions. "Get on," she pleaded with the girl. "They won't touch you if you're with me. You have my word on that." She eyed the enslavers striding their way, noting how they slowed when the girl clambered onto the back of the cart.

The girl slipped as she scaled the sacks of flour. The topmost sack slid beneath her bare foot, gliding majestically downward.

"Watch out!" Alla turned, the warning springing from her lips as swiftly as the sack tumbled to the ground.

It barely missed striking a palace guard in the process, the man diving to one side. He hoisted himself off the ground, clearly uninjured as he brushed the dust off himself. And with him dressed in all his finery, to boot.

My flour. Had she just lost one? And after all that haggling for a better quality. Alla knelt to examine the damage. A dusting of flour outlined the sack, but it didn't look like it had burst.

The sudden stop must've already upset the load. Nothing for it now but to lug the thing back onto the cart and hope it stayed there.

Standing, Alla turned on her heel and collided straight into a body with the unforgiving solidness of armour.

"Watch yourself, Missy." The man glared at her, his brows lowering.

Alla stepped back, realising she had bumped into the same palace guard. "My utmost apologies, good sir." Hastening to ensure her ears were covered, she curtsied deeply with her skirts spread wide. "I didn't mean to—"

The guard's brows lowered further, shading his eyes.

"Excuse me." She struggled to lift the sack. "I'll just—"

"My lady?" called out a light, almost breathy, voice.

The guard stiffened and saluted, his attention torn from Alla to whoever had spoken behind her.

Still wrestling with getting the sack of flour off the ground, she twisted to see what had garnered the guard's interest.

A woman, garbed in the finest shirt and trousers of pale blue silk Alla had ever seen, stood before them. Her dark eyes flicked from the guard to Alla and back. "Is there a problem here?"

The guard straightened and saluted. "I was just about to deal with this girl who attacked me."

"Attacked?" The woman smiled and something in Alla's chest fluttered. "I dare say she looks far too stunned to have done anything so brash. Are you all right, my lady? Do you need assistance?"

"No, thank you. I'm perfectly fine." Alla hoisted the sack off the ground, her arms objecting to being almost pulled from their sockets. The extra weight had her staggering back a few steps before she righted herself. "See? I've got—" The sack tumbled from her grasp to plop unceremoniously back onto the cobbles. "—it."

"Yes, I do see," the woman murmured, clearly fighting to keep her expression neutral. "Allow me." She waved her hand and the sack rose from the ground. It twisted, flattening out, to settle on top of the cart.

Envy briefly flashed through Alla's veins. If only she hadn't that blasted chain around her neck, then *she* could've done that. "Thank you," she mumbled, recalling her manners. With the high neckline of her dress, the woman couldn't possibly know that Alla's magic was contained. "I must be off now."

"Wait," the woman commanded. "I don't often come across nobles prepared to collect their own wares. Can you not linger awhile? I would very much like to talk."

Noble? It had been a long time since anyone new had taken her for more than a merchant's servant.

Alla turned to face the woman. With her thoughts no longer focused on the sack of flour, her mind fizzled at the sight even as her cheeks swiftly heated.

The woman was more than well-dressed. She held herself with a hypnotic combination of strength and elegance. Unlike the tree-like tallness of the surrounding humans, she came very close to Alla's height, although the woman lacked the same leanness. Her shoulders were quite broad, more so than her hips and the sleeves of her shirt was tight enough to show the sculpting effect of a warrior's training.

Whilst the blue silk of her outfit was heavily embellished in silver embroidery, her long angular face was somewhat less adorned. No powders or ink graced her ebony skin. No rings touched her narrow nose or her rather small and rounded ears. There were several clasps in her hair, though, and the rope-like twists of her locs were held back from her face by a fancy cord.

Judging by the stance and the guard's reaction, Alla guessed the woman was at least a captain in the royal guard. Or perhaps a noblewoman and likely well above the rank of countess that Alla's mother had once claimed.

The woman's square jaw was skewed in a refined smugness, the bottom half of those full lips captured by incredibly pristine teeth as if—

"Your highness," the guard said, snapping the thrall Alla had managed to fling herself under. "Is this little diversion really—?"

"*Highness?*" Panic lodged itself into Alla's throat. She knew of only one highness in the empire. The tsar had but one child. *The prince.* All this time, she'd been in the presence of the heir apparent? The jewel of Niholia's crown?

"Call me Vik."

The very idea of speech fled her senses. She wouldn't have dared utter the name even if it hadn't. Although words wouldn't come to her, Alla was able to shake her head. *Vik...* No doubt short for Prince Viktor.

The prince's head tilted to one side. "Then how about telling me *your* name?"

"I'm—" Alla glanced away before her tongue got the better of her. "I'm nobody important." Gathering her skirts, she scrambled onto the cart and urged the camels to move. "I really must be off. They're expecting me back home. My thanks for the help!"

The prince trotted leisurely beside her. "Are you coming to the ball?"

"The ball?" Alla squeaked.

"Yes. *My* ball. You *do* have an invitation, don't you?"

Alla failed to stifle a scoff, disbelief paralysing her tongue. Why would *she* have an invite to the ball? What would she do with one? No one wanted a half-breed there.

"Is that a no?" The genuine shock in the prince's voice almost had Alla stopping the cart. No one could actually think she was worthy of being in their presence, could they? "Ivan, one of the letters, if you please."

"But, your highness," gabbled a man that Alla only now realised was struggling to match the same pace as them. "His majesty's decree clearly states that only young women of a certain calibre are—"

The prince gave a throat-clearing cough. "Are you insinuating that this young lady is not to that standard?" Snatching a small scroll from a bag slung from the man's shoulder, the prince leapt onto the cart.

Alla froze. This couldn't be happening. If her stepmother found out she'd been talking to the prince, that she had allowed royal hands to touch this cart...

"Here." The prince thrust the scroll towards her. "Now, you can't say you've no invite."

Terror tightened her grip on the reins. Was she actually expected to take the blasted scroll whilst the prince clung on like a limpet? "Your highness," she finally managed. "I cannot possibly accept." She shook her head, desperate to make her stance known.

Clambering across the cart and grinning like a buffoon, the prince settled into next to her in the driver's seat. "Are you refusing a royal wish, my lady?"

Alla gasped. "Of course not, your highness. I—"

"Then, you can accept this." The prince pressed the scroll into Alla's hand. "And I *do* hope you will come. I'll be expecting to see you there."

The same warmth in her cheeks from earlier returned to invade her whole face. Before she could muster any semblance of an answer, the prince leapt from the cart to roll across the cobbles and spring upright before disappearing into the crowd like something from a fever dream.

Chapter 4

Alla plodded down the spiralling stairs with trays of dirty dishes carefully balanced before her. The smell of leftovers tweaked her nose and set her stomach to grumbling. *Gravy.* She pressed her lips together, staving off the idea of licking the plate where she stood. It had been so long since she'd eaten more than the claggy remains of someone else's meal.

Serving dinner, Alla's ears were assaulted by the same banter as the last two days, deviating from the coming ball only by the smallest of tweaks to the conversation. There had also been fewer complaints about their meal since Alla had set out everything before anyone sauntered into the study.

She was quite chuffed with her efficiency there, especially after such an exciting day. *Meeting the prince.* She never would've dared to dream of such a thing and still couldn't believe it to be real.

Ultimately, the evening meal ended the same as always. Her stepmother and stepsisters ate until they were near to bursting, then they left Alla to remedy whatever mess they made in the process.

The whole time, the invite burned in the back of Alla's mind.

She had considered throwing it from the cart the moment her and the girl had left the city, but couldn't bring herself to. There was something about the way the prince's smile set her stomach fluttering. A strange sensation. Almost a hunger.

I'll be expecting to see you there. The prince's words danced in her mind, so smooth and breathy.

It had taken a fair bit of restraint not to blurt out the news of what had transpired within the market to the trio. Not of the invite, and certainly not of the girl currently sitting in the kitchen, but a nasty little part of her wanted to gloat about meeting the prince, especially the part where the prince had pursued her and leapt aboard her cart.

Even if they believed her, she would be punished. Be it for bragging, for not mentioning her stepsisters to the prince, for the audacity of thinking she was worthy of a royal's time. Never mind that she had barely spoken a few words and had attempted to leave the prince behind.

Reaching the bottom of the stairs, she shuffled in the small space between the wall and the door to back through the kitchen entrance. The heavy door issued little more than the smallest of creaks as it swung inwards. Humid warmth hit her skin and sweat prickled across her upper lip.

Despite everyone else having eaten, the kitchen still bustled with activity. It would calm down once everyone was settled and ready to sleep, but for now, people worked with the goal of making tomorrow easier for each other.

The head cook had already shuffled off to his bed. With him no longer keeping his beady eyes on them, Uda shifted from shambling old woman to overseer of a much younger trio making bread dough. It would sit next to the dampened stove, proving and ready for baking tomorrow.

Others cleaned the benches or arranged the pantry. All whilst shuffling from foot to foot as the twins mopped the floor around them.

The girl Alla had met in the marketplace sat on an upturned barrel, watching everything with the same wide-eyed wariness.

During their travel back home, Alla had learnt the girl's name was Mady. Whether it was merely a piece of her name or not, Alla was relieved she remembered enough of her mother's teachings when it came to signing. She hadn't even registered that the girl hadn't spoken a word until Mady started using her good hand to answer the question, spelling out her name.

The kitchen staff happily welcomed Mady into the house, seeing her washed and garbed in the shorn off remains of someone's underdress. Her forearm was bandaged and nestled neatly in a sling, a broken bone being the consensus. Fractured, at the very least. What Alla had thought as grubby patches in her original cursory glance of the limb had actually been the beginning of bruising.

Small wonder she had run from the enslavers. They were probably the ones responsible for it.

Grumbling to herself, Alla plonked her trays next to the sink. After scraping every last bit of food from the dishes, she rolled up her sleeves and set about scrubbing them clean. It wasn't exactly something she was tasked with, but with Odette's injuries still hampering her ability to work, it was the least Alla could do.

She made swift work of the job and swiftly turn her attention to her usual nightly task of helping with the fireplace.

Yedivy glanced up as she knelt next to him, smiling his thanks. The scarring across his face—caused by an accident involving molten glass and an explosion—puckered his right cheek and set his face into a permanent smirk.

It was through him that Alla had learnt just how the glass barons made their money.

They worked together, Yedivy tackling one side of the massive hearth whilst she scrubbed the other. Old as it was, the fireplace needed more than their ministrations. Something was surely stuck in the chimney, for it haphazardly belched smoke whenever it was in use, covering everything in soot, including her skirts. But without someone sticking a pole up there to dislodge it, limiting its use to her stepmother's meals and tidying the mess was the next best thing.

Yedivy nudged her as she turned her attentions to the base of the hearth. He jerked his head in the direction of Mady. "What are you going to do with her? She can't exactly sneak by as being small for an adult." Beyond Mady, he was the youngest in the kitchen. Although not much younger than Alla's own twenty-one years, his injuries had aged him. Elves, at least the pure-blooded ones, could be quite small. Few reached five foot. She wasn't entirely sure that even *she* did, but Yedivy certainly did not, being that the top of his head barely reached her shoulder.

"I don't know yet." Keeping her hidden was as far as her

plan had gone. Mady needed time for her wrist to set. If she was discovered before then, her age wouldn't matter.

Somehow, Alla needed to convince her stepmother that the girl was actually an adult. Most humans had trouble determining the age of elven people. Added to Mady's taller-than-average height for her apparent age of seven... there was a slim chance. The alternative was to ensure the girl remained hidden at all times.

Yedivy sucked in a breath and looked as though he was about to say something else when the outer kitchen door creaked open.

Odette limped her way in. The other serfs halted in their work, parting before her. One of the twins scrambled to fetch a stool for the woman whilst the other supported Odette's every step.

Alla grabbed a freshly damp cloth from the sink and hastened to the woman's side. "Let me see how bad it is."

Odette waved Alla away as if the only thing ailing her was weariness. "I'll live, my lady. Not my first time under the lash."

"But you're not getting any younger." Elves might mend quicker than humans, but every time she was punished this way, it always took a little longer. And the risk of infection grew with it. Alla had seen such an ailment eat away at her favourite old camel. She didn't want that fate for anyone, especially not those dear to her.

Peeling back the fabric revealed the skin beneath to be dark and swollen. Welts crisscrossed the old woman's back, not deep enough to break the skin, but close. The only solace was that it hadn't been her stepmother's work. Her lashes were precise and often drew blood.

This was likely done by the serf master with an actual whip rather than magic.

Alla pressed the damp cloth to Odette's back, pursing her lips as the woman flinched. There was little she could do herself to actually soothe the woman. *If I could use my magic...* She fiddled with the chain. Even without the impediment, healing was an art that required years of study and refinement. She had been given no chance at garnering either.

Uda clicked her tongue. "I'll see to her, my lady." Even though her voice was strong, her hands still shook.

"Go get the stable master," Alla ordered over her shoulder, glaring at the group until one of them scuttled off. "Don't worry," she said to Odette, laying a hand on the woman's shoulder. "If anyone has something for the pain, it'll be him." Whether he would be inclined to hand any over was another matter.

"I'm not worried about me, my lady." Odette's gaze flicked to Uda, then back. The expression they shared was heavy, although the meaning behind it obscure to Alla.

"I don't know why you stay," Uda muttered as Alla returned to scrubbing the kitchen hearth. "*We* don't have a choice." She fiddled with her collar, her fingers tapping on the metal plate. "Such is our lot in life. But *you?*" The old woman shook her head. "You could—"

"*You* could still your tongue," Odette snapped. "If the Mistress caught wind of your words, she would cut it right out."

Wiping the sweat from her forehead, Alla sat back on her heels. "Why would I leave my father's estate fully under her thrall?" And where could she go that a half-breed would be treated better?

Maybe things would've been different if her father was still alive. He wouldn't have stood idly by whilst his second wife ruined his home and all-but-enslaved his daughter. He never would've married the woman if he had known, Alla was certain of it.

But what could she do that she hadn't already done? Her back had multiple reminders of what happened when she pushed against her stepmother's wishes.

Her supporting hand slid upon the hearth tiles, still wet with soap. The invite slipped from her apron pocket and rolled across the hearth, stopping in the grate. Alla hastened to shove it back, pushing the scroll deep into the corner of her pocket.

I'll be expecting... The prince's words echoed in the back of her mind as her fingers lingered on the scroll.

Shaking her head, Alla returned to her task. It didn't matter if the prince expected her, she couldn't go. How would she get there? In the carriage with her stepmother and stepsisters?

A snort erupted out her nose at the very idea. The noise garnered her a side-eyed stare from Yedivy, but little else. He likely thought dust had gotten up her nostrils.

Her nose tingled at the thought. A sneeze would come soon enough if she lingered on the idea. She knew from experience that any such blast of air would send up a cloud of soot.

Furiously rubbing the tip of her nose on the back of her hand, Alla turned to laying down fresh tinder and kindling for the fire. A few strikes of the flint sprayed sparks across the dried grass.

She sat back as tiny fingers of flames danced through the kindling. *Not too high.* It was a constant battle, keeping the flames low enough to avoid the fireplace belching smoke and passersby noticing the light through the kitchen window, but not so low that it died. But maintaining the fire within that little margin kept the night chill out of their bones.

Alla stared into the fire as those in the room slowly finished their tasks. Much like the growing flames, her thoughts flared and sputtered.

Even if some miracle allowed her the means to travel the distance to the palace, what would she wear? Certainly not any of the clothes she had altered for herself over the years. None of her stepsisters' donations would be sufficient, either.

She could try one of her mother's old dresses. She had packed away all the ones that weren't suitable for doing labour in a chest. There had to be something of use. Whatever she chose would undoubtedly need airing after years of storage and take a while to alter. But she had a week until the ball. She could do the work after everything else.

I shouldn't.

Alla dipped her hand into her apron pocket, closing upon the scroll. She should throw the blasted thing into the fire and be done with it. No invite. No temptation.

"My lady," a familiar voice murmured, drawing Alla from her thoughts. Gerde scuttled over with a small book, its leather cover cracked and flaking from neglect. "You've time to read it, haven't you?"

"Of course." She settled next to the fireplace, angling the book enough to catch the light. It was harder this way, and gave her a dreadful headache, but whilst the fire was low, Alla's eyesight was elven enough to let her see the words as if she stood in full sunlight.

Not that she needed to see. She must've read this tale a

hundred times.

The susurration of cloth sighed throughout the room as the others settled on the floor, some pillowing their heads in the laps of others or wrapping themselves tightly in their skirts.

Alla leafed through the book. "Where did I leave off?"

Gerde shuffled closer. Her head twisted as if trying to read as Alla continued skimming. "I believe it was just after the maiden finally met the prince, my lady." A murmur of agreement from the rest followed the woman's words.

Of course. Alla found the page easily enough. It was one of a few marked by a meticulous illustration that had grown dull with age and the constant tracing of the lines by idle fingers.

In the tale, the wise and gentle prince had taken the kind maiden as his bride. It was a hollow fantasy, or so her stepmother claimed. Nothing to be taken seriously. Like the idea of Alla going to the ball.

But the maiden in the story had managed it.

So why shouldn't *she* try?

Chapter 5

This is it. Alla clutched the invitation tightly to her chest as she stared into the mirror. She barely recognised the woman looking back, and it had nothing to do with the fractures in the silver-backed glass. With her hair artfully curled to frame her heart-shaped face and hide her ears, she could almost forget she wasn't fully human.

There was a hint of the grubby half-elven servant lingering in her gaze, though. A touch of uncertainty and fear as muddy as her eyes.

No. Alla squeezed her eyes shut. She heard enough of that from her stepsisters, she wasn't about to do it to herself. *Not mud*. Yes, they were the same colour, but that was also the shade of nuts, of seeds, of trees, of fertile soil in the early spring. *Of life*. That's what her father used to say. She was of the earth. And the earth was not some passive entity.

If she were the cowed little thing her stepmother thought her to be, she wouldn't have achieved as much in the time she had.

Every night, hour after hour whilst others slept, she had worked away at her mother's old wedding gown. The adjustments had taken more time than she had originally planned, largely due to her stepsisters' insisting she help them with their gowns. Based on the measurements their mother sent to the seamstress, their outfits had been too small.

She was almost grateful for the extra work. It gave her the opportunity to sneak thread into the attic without anyone wondering what she could possibly be using it for. And she had done it. The first step towards getting into the ball.

Alla gave a little twirl before the mirror, quite chuffed with the result of her work.

Style-wise, the dress was simple—high at the neck with a delicate petal motif in swooping layers around her waist. The fabric was a golden wheat shade that reminded Alla of her mother's hair in the sun. The skirt was topped by a layer of lace as fine as a spider's web. There was also a matching cape, although it barely managed to cover her shoulders.

She ran a hand down the front, the roughness of her fingers catching on the lace. Everything was so delicate that she had first dismissed the idea of attempting an alteration, but nothing else had spoken to her like this. Wearing it almost felt like she took a piece of her mother with her. *To the ball.*

There was just one more hurdle she needed to clear.

Her gaze slid to the attic entrance. The hatch sat closed for now even though no one but her ever ventured up here. Alla lifted the heavy wooden panel. The stairs seemed to go on forever in the darkness.

She might've worked her fingers to the bone to prepare herself for tonight, but her stepmother could stop everything.

Alla took a steadying breath as she descended the attic stairs. She had rehearsed every possible scenario in her head until her mind spun. She'd an answer for every logical reason her stepmother might refuse her simple request to go with them to the palace.

She padded through the empty rooms, her bare feet silent on the rugs. What little noise there was came from below. Everyone would be roped in to see the trio off and would do so gladly for the chance of a night without their presence.

"Do hurry it along, girls," her stepmother said.

Alla's hand tightened on the invitation. She tucked the scroll into a small pocket stitched into the skirt. All through the week, the invite had been her proof that this wasn't a dream. Now, it was her only way through the palace doors.

If her stepmother found it…

I can do this. Taking a deep breath, she pushed open the upper door to the foyer and descended the first few steps. Having helped Tamara into her gown only a short while ago, she knew precisely when the trio were leaving. If she was going to join them, it had to be now.

"Honestly," her stepmother groaned. "The last thing we want to be is behind all the riffraff."

The trio stood in the middle of the foyer. Her stepmother seemed preoccupied with directing this or that person to fetch what was required, all whilst trying to herd her daughters towards the front door. None of them paid much attention to each other or the people rushing after their every whim, never mind Alla's presence.

Standing halfway up the stairs, she cleared her throat.

Her stepmother paused in ordering a different colour shawl and glanced over her shoulder. "Speaking of riffraff..." She eyed Alla up and down. "*What* are you wearing?"

"My mother's old wedding gown?" She glanced down at the swathes of old silk and gauzy lace. "I... fitted it myself. At night, after all my chores," she hastily added before she was accused of being negligent with her tasks. "I thought that, maybe, I could—?"

"Go to the ball?" Natalya blurted. "Is that what you were going to say? How preposterous." She laughed, a dreadfully harsh sound, and nudged her sister. "Can you imagine?"

"Does Little Soot want to dance with the scullery boys?" Tamara cackled away as if it were a great joke. "And with no shoes, too."

Alla self-consciously rubbed her feet together. Going without footwear wasn't exactly a choice. She didn't have any shoes and no one else in the household wore them in her size.

Through all her stepsisters' laughter, her stepmother merely stared at Alla, her face tight. Alla doubted the tinge of red flushing her stepmother's cheeks was rouge.

"I won't get in anyone's way," Alla promised as she trotted down a few more steps. "I just want to see—"

"After everything I have given you?" her stepmother said, the words barely louder than a serpent's sigh in the grass. "You dare?"

"I only wish to see the palace. I don't even want to meet anyone." That she had already spoken with the prince was enough, even if those few words had been little more than squeaks of protest. "I won't talk to anyone who doesn't address me first. I won't fuss or make a scene."

"No, you most certainly won't," her stepmother agreed. "Because you're not going."

"But everyone of noble birth is invited and I—" She closed her mouth with a click, almost biting her tongue, before she blurted the rest of the words. *I'm expected.* She curled her fingers around the invitation still tucked into her pocket. It took all her willpower not to clutch the scroll before her like a shield.

"Noble? *You?*" Scoffing, her stepmother strode closer. She planted herself before Alla, one hand on her hip. "Look at you. Those rags aren't even fit to grace a corpse, never mind be seen by royal eyes. Why, I bet they would fall apart at the slightest touch." She reached out, her fingers clawed.

Alla jerked back. She had worked too hard, for too many nights, to see her efforts destroyed. "My mother's clothes are not rags." She clutched the skirts. "This was her wedding dress." Neither of her parents would've walked into the temple in anything less than their best.

"Your mother was an *elf*, child," her stepmother snapped, speaking in that slow tone she used on the rest of the household. "What else would she possibly wear?"

"She was married to my father. She was a countess." Just as Alla was. There would be documents out there stating that fact, although she'd no clue where or how to access them.

Her stepmother laughed. "Your mother was a disgrace and embarrassment. And *you?* You are lower than common, dear girl. You're a half-breed that even your father knew better than to tout. I wouldn't be seen around a *dog* with such mixed breeding, never mind a person."

"My father loved my mother." Her memories of her parents together were few and clouded with age, but she remembered light and love. He had never been anywhere near that happy after her mother's death. Perhaps longing for that in his life again was what had driven him to seek out her stepmother. "Which is more than I can say about his motives in marrying *you.*"

Colour drained from her stepmother's face. She looked Alla over as if they had never met before.

Pain lanced across Alla's right cheek, magic the only source.

She pressed a hand to the spot. Warmth soaked into her fingertips. No blood. A warning blow.

"Poisonous little runt," her stepmother hissed, storming up the stairs even as Alla retreated. "Do you honestly think I would want my daughters associated with a half-breed? You're lucky I don't toss you out on the street this instant for your insolence."

"Mother," Tamara called from the front entrance. "We're going to be late."

"Only fashionably, dear. Nothing to be concerned about. I just need to deal with this first. It won't take long."

"Can't you punish her when we get back?" Natalya asked. She also lingered by the door, two equally ghastly shawls in her arms.

"Yes," Alla muttered. "It isn't as though they're going to shut the gates after the sun has set." She had caught that little snippet of information in the market square.

"Mother!" Tamara stomped her foot and glared up at them before looking outside.

"Hush, you silly goose. She doesn't know what she's talking about."

"No," Alla replied, unable to contain the bitterness coating her tongue. "I couldn't possibly have heard such details from the palace crier whilst buying your food."

"And you didn't think to tell us?" Her stepmother lunged for her, clutching the front of Alla's dress like a hawk with a fish. The fabric strained, tightening at the back of Alla's neck.

She fought to get loose. Physically, she was smaller than her stepmother, but also stronger. And yet, the woman's hold remained firm. *Magic.* Her stepmother had to be using her healing gifts to boost her strength. There was no other way she could be restraining Alla with such ease. It wouldn't last. The power would tear her stepmother apart if the woman tried.

Alla adjusted the dress waist. She just had to hold still until—

The scroll slipped from her pocket. In one frantic burst of might, Alla wrenched herself free of her stepmother's grasp and dove for the scroll as it bounced and rolled down the stairs.

Her stepmother's magic got there first.

"What is this?" Her stepmother lifted the scroll into her

grasp. "An invite?" Her brows drew together as she perused the words. "A *personal* one? How did you get this?" She shook it at Alla. "Answer me, girl."

"It was given to me."

"You?" Her stepmother laughed. "Liar! Who would gift anything to a worthless little half-breed? You must have stolen it. From one of them?" She pointed at her daughters.

"No, I—" Alla fell silent as her feet left the ground. Bands of air solidified around her, threatening to crush her bones where she floated. Not once had her stepmother used more than a few lashes of magic to quell her in the past.

In a breathless rush, she found herself flying into her stepmother's grasp.

"What else have you been stealing?" Heat radiated from the woman's hand and the stench of scorched silk invaded Alla's nose. "I kept you here. I followed your father's wishes, against my better judgement. I raised you alongside my daughters and this is how you repay me?" She held up the scroll.

Flames licked along the outer coil of parchment, blackening the edges and spreading. Her stepmother dropped the scroll along with her hold on Alla, leaving it to crumple to the floor.

The parchment flaked and crumbled as it fluttered to the tiles.

"No!" Alla fell to her knees, smothering the flames with her skirt in an effort to put out the fire. "Please no." She had only meant to go for a little while. *I'm expected.*

When she withdrew the soot-stained silk, only ashes and a puddle of wax remained.

"Stop blubbering," her stepmother snapped. "Be grateful I haven't cut off your hands. I should for your thievery, but you're of better use to me intact."

Alla cradled the remains. She had been so close. "Why?" she whispered. "Why do this? What harm would it have done to let me go?"

Her stepmother grabbed Alla's chin in a bruising grip. "I'm going to let you in on a little secret, child. You weren't meant to exist."

Alla frowned.

"Everyone knows that half-breeds aren't cut from the same divine cloth as pure children. They're the work of demons.

They're mistakes."

"That's not true."

"It is. Your father ignored all the warnings leading to his death. He allowed his head to be turned by some pretty property that wasn't even his." Latching onto Alla's wrist, she hauled Alla to her feet and marched up the stairs. "Even you coming into the world wasn't enough to convince him into changing his ways."

They strode through the same rooms and hallways Alla had trodden on her way down from the attic. Was that where the woman planned to take her?

Alla couldn't have that.

She planted herself and tugged. They stumbled for a step, her stepmother almost releasing her hold before clamping down hard enough to make Alla's hand go numb.

"And because of his sinful ways," her stepmother continued. "Your father made a mockery of me. But my parents were fortunate enough to find another suitor. A more powerful one."

"I don't understand," Alla confessed. "What—?"

"Your father was supposed to marry me."

"No." She knew little of her grandparents and had never met them. They had been old even when her father had been quite young and insisted he marry before they passed on. Not once had her father mentioned an arranged marriage.

They halted at the attic entrance. "He paid for his slight on my person. His sin was purged in the fires of war. But *you...*" She glanced over her shoulder, coolly arching an eyebrow. "You have yet to pay for your sins. I shan't have you embarrassing me any further." She pushed Alla ahead of her.

Alla stumbled up the stairs, catching her footing barely in time to keep herself from sprawling onto the floor. She whirled on the woman.

Her stepmother stood in the attic, planted before the entrance.

"All this time, you've been punishing me for what my father did? For him choosing the woman he loved over *you?*" What had possessed her father to marry the woman in the end? Guilt? Pity?

"For choosing sin over duty. For not learning his place. Your mother should've known it. She should've stayed where she belonged. And your father was raising you to be the same, to believe in fairy tales and happy endings." She pressed so close that their noses almost touched. "They don't exist, child. Certainly not for little half-breeds."

Balling her hands, Alla faced the woman square on. Her father had done more than believe in fairy tales. He had done his best to be fair and treat all people, human or elven, with kindness, especially those who relied on him. That was what both her parents had wanted in her, kindness and bravery. She tried every day to live up to that expectation.

Right now, she struggled to embrace either.

Her stepmother stepped back, keeping Alla firmly in sight even as she descended the steps. "I shall deal with your attitude in the morning. Now, stay in there and I might forget your insolence. And think about how lucky you are that I don't cut out your tongue this instant." The hatch slammed shut.

In the stillness that followed, the soft grate of a lock echoed through the attic.

Alla dropped to her knees. An aching hollowness settled in her chest and trickled down her cheeks. She took in the remains of her mother's old wedding dress, the tattered and soot-stained skirts, the scorched fabric at the breast. *Rags*. Was that really all she was fit to wear?

Maybe her stepmother was right. No matter how hard Alla fought for what she wanted, something always came around to block her chances at being happy. Even if that happiness was only for a little while.

Maybe she wasn't meant to be happy.

Maybe it was time to give up.

Chapter 6

Alla sat curled up before the small painting of her mother. She didn't often have time to do more than glance at the artwork, always looking without really taking in what she saw. Never had she truly gazed upon it, not even in the daylight. Under the waning, flickering light of a candle stub, the intricate brush strokes and soft touches of gilding that made up the portrait had her mother looking almost like another person.

It was hard to imagine her mother's pale face blistering and burnt from the sun or the utter disarray of her usually immaculate golden hair. But even in the painting, her mother looked so frail. Not frightened, not since Alla's father had helped her escape. Just fragile.

Be brave and remember who you are. Those were the last words her mother had uttered to her before the horse ride that broke her neck. Alla had been preparing for her debut at court, learning the dances, the mannerisms, what to do if anyone of higher ranking spoke to her.

Alla had rather flubbed the last one.

Her mother wouldn't have stumbled over her words so terribly. Although frail in looks, she had started off life as a slave. The slight scarring around her neck was obvious in the portrait. She hadn't been like the other elven women here, belonging to the family estate and destined to become her father's property, whether he wanted them or not. Nor had she been the spoils from a clash with a rival family.

The tale her parents told her of their meeting had been a

simple one, cut down to the basics to answer a child's questions. Her mother had been fleeing a glass baron. Even back then, Alla hadn't needed to ask why. They never said which one, though. Sometimes, Alla wondered if either of them even knew anything of the man beyond the obvious.

Her mother had darted down a side street to avoid the enslavers. That was when they had stumbled into each other, literally colliding in the market square before her mother coerced her father into hiding her.

The meeting was all it had taken for her father to fall, the sort of love he wished for his daughter one day. She knew it in the depths of her soul.

Her stepmother was right about one thing, happily ever after didn't come for half-breeds like her. Not like in the stories. They were always full-blooded humans and typically spellsters who had either been tricked into giving up their magic or had stumbled into a place where it didn't work.

Whereas Alla...

She sniffed, trying to choke back a fresh welling of tears. Thanks to her stepmother, she would never know more than this little plot of dying land.

Why had her father married the woman? Had he not known her to be the same one he had chosen Alla's mother over? That seemed unlikely. It must've been guilt. For her stepmother? For her?

And what of her stepmother's words? *Paying for his slight.* Did she mean the marriage or worse? Could she be responsible for the death of Alla's mother? *She couldn't have.* Her mother's death had been an accident.

Although...

It wasn't hard to spook a horse. Enough to ensure an experienced rider fell off? That was also relatively simple. But to have that same person break their neck in the process? It would be tricky, but not impossible. If only she had proof.

The subtle groan of wood from outside the attic door broke her musing. Someone had stepped onto the stairs leading up here. Alla barely acknowledged the creak of the little hinges as that same person tried the hatch. Whoever it was would be aware she was locked within. It wasn't as if her stepmother would be home until the early hours of the morning, not if things went well for her and her daughters.

"My lady," Uda called from the other side of the door, her customary no-nonsense tone echoing through the attic. "It's time to stop snivelling and get ready."

"Get ready for what?" she snapped back. Where could she possibly be headed that rags wouldn't suffice?

"The ball!" Odette called from somewhere far outside.

Alla opened the attic window wider.

The old woman stood out in the yard, a lit lantern held high. "If you hurry, child, you can make it before the gates close."

Not on foot she couldn't. Via cart or carriage, perhaps. But that was a minor issue in comparison. "In this mess?" She tugged at the tattered skirts of her dress as if either woman could see. "You must be joking."

"Of course not in your ruined clothes," Uda scoffed.

"Come down, my lady," Odette insisted. "We have it all in hand."

Down? Alla peered at the mansion wall, searching for her usual footholds. In the hazy light of late afternoon, the way seemed to stretch on for eternity. Never had she needed to climb down the wall before. What if she misjudged and fell? She could suffer a lot worse than a broken neck.

"Quickly," Uda snapped from the other side of the door. The creak of the step swiftly followed. Had she gone to find a means to open the hatch? Or was she headed off to wait below?

Alla swung out onto the windowsill. In all her times scurrying up, not once had she considered the drop. *Be brave.* She'd gone up dozens of times. Surely, down just required a little more care.

Gripping the ledge, she lowered herself. Her feet dangled in the air, finding nothing before her toes brushed the rooftop.

Down she went, slower than a snail in the summer heat. Each step came blindly as she relied on wedging her toes into every minuscule crack. She clung to every lip and outcrop, digging in wherever she could. Looking down to see how far she had left wasn't an option, so she stuck to treating any moment, any misstep, as the potential to be her last.

Finally, there was only the jump from the top of the stone water tub to the ground. Her legs wobbled as she landed, relief weakening her muscles. She let out a trembling breath as she gazed up the way she'd come. It seemed higher in the twilight.

"Hurry, hurry." Odette hopped from one foot to the other. She shooed Alla inside through the nearby kitchen door. "To your stepsisters' dressing room. We really haven't much time if we're getting you to this ball."

"I can't get there." She waved a hand at the barn where the carriage and cart were kept. Its doors were open and lights flickered within. No doubt the people were taking advantage of the space whilst waiting for the carriage's return. "What would I travel in?"

"Never you mind that," Odette said as she hustled Alla through the kitchen and up the spiralling stairway to the story above. The woman continued to guide Alla down the hall as if this was her first time stepping into the mansion. "I told you we've got it all in hand. You just worry about getting out of that dress and into something suitable."

"Like what?" Altering her mother's dress had taken days. Of all the remaining dresses that actually fitted her, it had been the only decent one.

Odette veered off into a suite that Alla had once known as her own. It now belonged to her stepsisters. It consisted of three rooms, one which had been Alla's study where she had learnt all manner of skills befitting a young noblewoman, from court etiquette to a rudimentary study of farm management and even idle skills such as painting or reclining to read.

Her stepsisters had turned it into a massive wardrobe. The racks brimmed with gowns, from simple dresses of dyed linen to those with elaborate silk brocade. Together, the pair had thrice as many of the latter than all the outfits Alla had ever owned in her life.

Uda stood in the middle of the room, not far from a small podium and the massive standing mirror. She held up an overdress Alla vaguely remember Tamara wearing as a young teenager. "This should fit you close enough, my lady."

The main body of the overdress was dark green with a slightly lighter hue on the gauzy sleeves and hem. Golden embroidery adorned the shoulders and breast, wide and plentiful at the top, then narrowing as it neared the waist. A shimmery, mustard brown underdress lay on a nearby stool, clearly designed to complement the rest of the attire.

I shouldn't. It was one thing to attempt sneaking into the ball, but if she was discovered by her stepmother? Whilst wearing one of her stepsister's gowns? The scars on her back ached just thinking about it.

The answer was simple. *Don't get caught.* The dress wouldn't be the only one this style or colour. If she remained vigilant, then she would spy the trio before they could make out her face.

Alla shucked the ruined layers of her gown until she stood in her undergarments. Her own underdress wasn't terribly singed and she would've kept it on had it not been longer than the green overdress. Whilst it had been perfectly adequate under her mother's old wedding gown, the dirty off-white shade would have people turning their heads for the wrong reasons.

Between the two old women and herself, Alla was able to swiftly don the new attire. It fitted loosely and sat awkwardly around her chest as she had rather less in that department to fill out the fabric.

Uda worked to tuck the excess, placing a few quick stitches at key points to hold everything in place. They led her to the stool where Odette combed Alla's hair whilst Uda finished fastening all the fiddly buttons that held the overdress closed at the chest.

Odette stood back, a tearful smile crinkling her blue eyes. "Look at you," she murmured, her voice strained, as she styled Alla's hair into the usual curls to hide her ears. "No longer the young girl I used to chase out of the stables. When did you grow up?"

"You look just like your mother," Uda added, securing the final button.

"Don't spout such lies." Odette cupped Alla's chin. "She's in there, rightly enough, but it's your father's gentle nature that I see peeking through those eyes. We just need something to finish off the look. Maybe a nice necklace or—"

"No!" The neckline of her borrowed attire was high enough to allow her the option of hiding the magic-nullifying necklace. But if anyone noted that purple chain, then it wouldn't matter how regal she looked. Avoiding anything that could draw attention to the area was also paramount. "Maybe I just shouldn't go."

There were so many risks that didn't involve her stepmother. If the chain was discovered, she could be accused of being a criminal or an escaped slave. If her ears were uncovered, she'd be seen as impersonating a human noble.

She lifted her head, staring defiantly at her own reflection. *I am noble.*

A pity no one would wait for her to explain that fact, never mind believe her title. But surely, if her mother could enter the palace at her father's side, then Alla could alone.

"What we *need*," Uda muttered, her head buried deep within the bottom row of shelves taking up the back wall. She unearthed box after box that couldn't have been shifted for years. "Are some shoes."

Alla laughed. She hadn't even thought of them. "I suppose going to the ball in bare feet isn't really an option." But where to find shoes that would fit? All the household serfs went around with feet as naked as her own and the few servants her stepmother employed didn't have anything respectable.

"Got them!" Uda cried out triumphantly as she trotted over with a wooden box. "I knew she hadn't tossed the blighters. They won't be a perfect fit, but they'll be the closest match to your size." Setting the box before Alla, she pulled out a pair of crystalline shoes.

Alla scrunched her bare toes into the plush rug. "I can't wear those. Where did you even find them?" They looked brand new. It was a big enough of a risk turning up at the ball in one of her stepsister's old dresses. To then borrow something they had yet to make use of? It was worth more than her life.

"Mistress had them commissioned for Lady Natalya," Uda replied, lifting one of the shoes higher. The woman's wrinkled and suntanned fingers were clearly visible through the body of the shoe. "Back when there was an influential glass baron from the western shore sniffing around her daughters. By the time these shoes arrived, they no longer fit."

Alla extended a leg and let Uda slip the shoe onto her foot. It was icy and just that little bit too loose, whatever grip it maintained came only from the friction against her skin.

Odette hummed over her shoulder. "Maybe some stockings will—"

"No," Uda said. "We've not the time." She practically

bounced onto her feet to grab Alla's hand. "Quickly now."

All three of them scampered out into the hall and down the front stairs. Her borrowed shoes slipped and clacked alarmingly after the first few frantic steps. Alla slipped off the shoes and carried them. Walking wouldn't be quite an issue. Dancing might, but she could easily stick to the slow ones.

They reached the front door and trotted into the yard where—

Alla froze, taking in the cart that was hitched and waiting for her. The same one she had driven to the market just a week ago in. Neither woman could possibly think they'd make it to the palace gates before they closed, could they? Personal experience told her it was nowhere near as fast as the carriage.

"Get in, my lady." Odette urged her onwards with a wave of a hand. "Just hop in the back and let us worry about getting you there in time." She scrambled into the driver's seat, assisting Uda up next to her.

Alla gently handed the shoes to Odette before tucking her skirts high and vaulting into the back of the cart.

Her feet had barely settled before Uda urged the camels forward at a flat run. The beasts wouldn't be able to maintain the pace the whole way, but they would definitely cover a great deal of distance.

Alla's heart leapt as the cart bounced and swayed along the road. The wind whipped at her hair, undoing all of Odette's work. Alla didn't care. Her chance to step inside the palace was really happening. She would finally see the world she had only ever dared to dream of for so many years. The one she denied to her for so long.

And no one was around to stop her.

Chapter 7

They clattered through the gates just as they were closing.
Uda shouted her apologies to the guards and something
that sounded like an explanation. With her gaze drawn to the
glittering palace entrance, Alla made out little of the woman's
words.

The sweeping path wound up between a double row of large
palms. Blue globes of magical light illuminated the way,
continuing up the wide stairs leading to the open door.
Carriages rolled ahead of them, pausing at the foot of the stairs
only for their passengers to emerge before the drivers urged the
horses on.

Alla strained to find the unadorned, glossy dark wood of her
stepmother's transport. Whilst she had considered the odds of
avoiding them within the palace walls, out here would be
harder. There were a few dark carriages, but nothing as plain
and none seemed to be pulled by camels.

She allowed herself to relax, taking the time to adjust her
attire and fix the mess the wind had made of her hair. Pins
held some of the curls in place, especially those over her ears.
She couldn't afford to be complacent about it, though. Letting
people know about the elven side of her heritage was always a
gamble and ending up in the palace dungeon, or worse, was not
on her agenda.

The cart rocked, unexpectedly turning and picking up pace.

Slipping her borrowed shoes, Alla glanced up to see their
passage veer away from the orderly line of carriages. "Where

are you going?" She lurched forward, draping herself over the seat between the two women. "The entrance is right there."

Uda shook her head. "I can't just drop you off the back of a cart like a sack of flour, my lady. Not at the front door. Not in this rickety thing." She urged the camels on with a gentle jiggle of the reins on the animals' rumps.

Off to the side, away from the front entrance, but within view of the stairs, sat the drivers with their carriages and harnessed horses. They chatted amongst themselves as the cart trundled by.

Alla scrunched herself further between the women. Somewhere amongst those drivers was one of the few servants her stepmother employed. Being human, he wouldn't be capable of picking out their faces in the gloom, especially with them backlit by the glowing palace entrance. But she also wasn't in the mood to push her luck.

"We'll go around the back," Uda continued as the cart left the smoothness of the flagstone path. It bumped and swayed through the gravel into the velvet darkness lurking beyond the light. "Where the stables are."

"And a servant's entrance," Odette added.

Alla pulled her gaze from the dwindling group of drivers to peer at the woman. "How do you know that?" Whilst it could be easily inferred that there would be other buildings beyond the one the royal family lived in, Odette spoke with the soft confidence of prior knowledge. Yet, she had been born into the family estate just as Alla had, albeit under vastly different circumstances.

Uda chuckled. "She's been here before. With your mother."

"You *have*?" Alla pushed herself further onto the seat.

"I really couldn't tell you much, child." Odette waved her hands as if trying to erase Alla's memory whilst glaring at a still-chortling Uda. "I saw little beyond a few rooms. You'll see far more, I'm certain. But don't worry about all of that right now. Just believe me when I say the servant entrance won't be locked. We'll see that you get inside, my lady."

Inside. If she entered the palace by any other door beyond the main one, everyone would expect her to have already been announced. *She'll never know I was here.* Alla had thought to give the announcer a false name, but this was better. If she didn't tell anyone who she was, then she couldn't be accused of pretending to be someone she wasn't.

Except she already was.

Alla glanced over her shoulder at the carriages all lined up. She had been looking forward to traversing the sweeping stairway to the main entrance, to be bathed in the magical glow of the lanterns, to lose herself in the chatter of those who didn't know her or her past, only that she was noble like them.

When the cart rounded the corner, the ethereal glow slipped from sight. The palace walls loomed over them, unwelcoming and dark beyond a single illuminated window several floors up. Another huge building sat off to the side. A stable or warehouse, she wasn't certain of which.

Uda pulled on the reins, slowing the camels' shuffling walk. They crept along, the cartwheels crunching in the gravel. The weak light of a single lantern lit a doorway tucked into the palace brickwork.

The cart came to a stop opposite the entrance. A set of steps led up to the closed door. *Small.* Nothing would be as grand as the palace's main point of entry, but this wasn't how she had pictured the other entrances to be. Where were the people? The bustle? Surely, not all the servants were in the palace.

"This'll lead you through to the lower levels," Odette said. "There's a winding stairway to the left that'll take you up to the main foyer."

Alla frowned. That way would likely be guarded. She would have to come up with a suitable lie for why she was in the palace's lower levels. Or maybe she could slip past them. There had to be more than one way up.

Gathering her skirts, she daintily stepped down from the cart.

Her foot had barely swung out over nothing when the shoe slipped from her foot. It hit the gravel, bouncing along the ground with a musical clink.

No! Hauling off the other shoe, Alla leapt from the cart after the fallen one. Had it broken? She was this close to the ball. With the gates no longer admitting entry, it wasn't a case of simply returning home and coming back. Besides, where would she get replacement footwear?

Odette reached the shoe first. The crystalline surface

glittered in the lantern light as the woman examined it.

Whole. Not even a hint of a chip. Alla's stomach fluttered, relief washing through her, making her queasy.

"Try to be careful, my lady." Odette helped her put the shoes back on.

"It seems I won't be doing much dancing," Alla said, laughing. Not that she had expected to. Never mind she knew only the court dances her father had taught her, simple ones that a small child could master. She doubted few would choose to be seen cavorting with an unknown woman.

Smiling in that trying-not-to-worry-Alla fashion that she so often did, Odette fussed with Alla's hair. "You'll have to find your own way out of the palace grounds." Those long fingers teased the curls into place over Alla's ears and smoothed whatever straggly bits that had come undone during their journey. "We'll wait for you near the gates until midnight, but no longer. If the mistress sees us..."

"I understand." Cupping Odette's elbow, Alla guided the woman back onto the cart. "You've already done so much for me. Both of you." Since the death of her father, these dear women had taken responsibility for Alla and kept her safe from situations that could see her sold off to some work team in the desert. "I don't know what I would do without either of you."

"Don't you worry about that, my lady." Uda urged her on with the limp flap of a hand. "Go. Enjoy yourself. And stay safe."

Be brave. Alla breathed deeply. This close to the ocean, the sea air permeated everything. "I will."

Gathering her skirts, she scurried up the steps and cautiously opened the door. The way forward was lit only by the lantern at her back. *Still no one.*

Alla paused in the doorway. Outside the darkness of her shadow, she caught the impression of shelves and barrels lining an otherwise straight path to another door. It seemed to hold nothing of note.

Confident she wouldn't trip over anything, she stepped deeper into the room.

The door swung shut, throwing everything into utter darkness for the few moments it took for her eyes to adjust. A sliver of light leaked under the door, but left her with little to go by. *Straight ahead*. As long as she kept on that path, she would reach the opposite wall.

She shuffled forward a few steps, her hand searching before her, her feet clacking on the bare stone floor. Inch by inch, she crossed the room. The time it took seemed endless. Would she leave here to find the night was over?

Her fingertips touched something cool. Another step brought her close enough to slap the surface with her palm. A wall. But which one?

Alla peered into the blackness. Impossible to tell. Looking back only told her she had left the entrance behind and that wasn't terribly helpful.

Laying both hands on the wall, she tapped the surface in search of a door or a corner. *Left first*. She had taken only a few steps before her skirts bumped against one of the barrels she had spied earlier.

Shuffling to her right, her hand landed on something icy lying flat against the wood. *Metal*. A little more exploration revealed it to be triangular. *A hinge?* That could only mean...

Alla felt further along, finding the gap between wood and stone, then following it up from the floor to where she expected a handle to be. A thin curve of metal with a simple latch greeted her questing fingers.

The hallway beyond wasn't as dark, allowing Alla to trot down the strip of carpet in the middle without fear of bumping into anything. Or anyone. Other corridors branched off, but she walked onwards in the hope that it was the right path.

She caught the distant chatter of people, ghostly murmurs of noise in the silent passageways. She couldn't pinpoint a direction. *Up*. That was where she needed to go, but there didn't appear to be any stairs, winding or otherwise.

Undeterred, she kept walking. The palace might be big enough to swallow several mansions, but it wasn't endless. If she couldn't find the way herself, then she would have to find a person.

What would she say to them? That she was lost? Possibly plausible once in the upper levels, but down here? She'd wager none of the nobility came anywhere near these halls.

More distinct murmurs reached her ears. Two voices, one deeper than the other and growing louder. The flickering light of a lantern danced around the corner, getting brighter with each step.

Alla froze in the middle of the corridor. Down here, it could easily be a servant rather than a guard. The former she could bluff and bluster her way by. But if it was the latter? For her to then declare herself lost wandering where no noble was expected to be?

"...and I told her ladyship..."

Panic stole her breath for a heartbeat. *I shouldn't have come.* No one knew she was here beyond Odette and Uda. And who would believe two serfs? *Nobody.* Nor would anyone notice she was missing except for them and a few others back at the mansion. Her stepmother certainly wouldn't care. She would likely be elated to find herself free of Alla.

The steadying grasp of reason took hold. She had paid attention to the turns, which meant she could retrace her path through these dismally dark corridors to the entrance. From there, it would be a simple matter of meeting up with the old women outside the palace gates.

No one would give her departure a second glance.

She wouldn't get to see the ballroom, though. Or any more of the palace gardens than the little they had driven by. Everything the two women had risked in getting her here would be for nothing.

"No, you didn't," the one with the deeper voice snapped at their companion. "Don't look at me like that. If you *had* told her that, then you'd be wearing your face on the inside right now." The steady tramp of their feet echoed alongside the voice.

Guards. Perhaps Odette had been wrong about this section of the palace.

Alla took a step back, her heel hitting bare stone instead of carpet. The clack of her shoes bounced up the corridor.

"What was that?"

Hopping from one foot to the other, Alla quickly snatched the shoes from her feet and scampered down the first side corridor she spied. She sped on, not willing to pause until she had rounded several bends and taken at least one fork in the passageway. Whilst the guards might've guided her to the ballroom, she had no guarantee that they would or of them not asking questions along the way. She wasn't ready to face questions.

Certain no one had followed, she flattened against the wall. Her ears strained over her rasping breath for the sound of pursuit. Nothing.

Clutching the shoes to her chest, she continued down the corridor. There were no rugs here and her bare feet slapped against the cool stone. She glanced back the way she had come. The carpet had vanished after the second corner. Or had that been the fourth? It had certainly been before the fork.

Looking ahead of her, she tilted her head. Light? She blinked several times, not sure if the passage was illuminated by the weak glow of stationary light or if her eyes were playing tricks on her.

She padded faster down the corridor, turning another corner to be faced with a winding flight of stairs. Light leaked from above. No sign of people. No music. No chatter. Not even a footstep. Perhaps that was for the best right now.

"Time to get my story straight," she murmured, peering down at the shoes. *A gift from a glass baron.* She might not know all the names, but there were a lot of them in the east, where the crystalline sand made for the finest glass creations. Could she get away with posing as the daughter of one?

"I am Lady Alla." That was how her father had taught her to address those within the court. Yet, the words fell stiffly from her lips. Odette still called her by that title, although Alla wasn't certain she could lay claim to it after her father's death.

Slipping the shoes on, she carefully ascended the stairs. How could she expect even the meekest of servants to believe her when she barely believed it? "I *am* Lady Alla." Better.

At the top of the stairs, light blue curtains covered the doorway. She pushed them apart and stepped into an illuminated hall. Not the narrow corridors she had just walked, but a huge chamber with gilded lanterns and great pillars supporting a vaulted ceiling.

Paintings lined both sides of the hall, mostly portraits of couples. Alla halted before the closest one. The man was obviously a tsar from ages past. Judging by the coronation dates on the plaque, these two would've been the current tsar's grandparents. *Such detail.* Her father had adored some of the painters of old and had spent a great many nights pointing out how even the tiniest of brush marks could lovingly mould an image.

The longer she admired the work, the more her eye was drawn to the woman.

Alla stared until her eyes began to water. It wasn't obvious at a casual glance as the portrait lacked the usual pointed features—her hair piled high in a style that suspiciously covered her ears. It was in her face and eyes. And in her hands? Lean, long fingers grasped an orb of marbled red and gold. Nothing about those digits said human.

The woman sitting beside the old tsar was elven.

It can't be. She stepped back, tracking along the portraits for the next generation, the old tsar who had ruled when Alla's father was a child. It was hard to pick out, most likely due to a product of artistic licence, but there were hints of something not entirely human about the old tsar.

She marched up and down in front of the portraits. It wasn't just that one woman. There were other elves amongst the paintings, all with their most prominent attributes hidden. It was a mere handful amongst dozens, and all women, but they sat right alongside that generation's ruler as if they belonged.

Shaking her head, Alla turned from the old paintings. She had to be imagining it. There were no noble elves. Maybe that one woman was a half-breed like herself or the artist had deliberately altered certain features to make it appear as though she might be in some sort of objection to the elven repression of old.

She halted before the final portrait. Tsar Petya, the current ruler. He appeared quite the serious example of royalty with the intense stare of his dark eyes and his brows set in a stern line. The slight curve of his mouth somewhat spoiled the imposing facade. The tsarina looked a little more composed, but not by much.

The tsar also held that strange marbled orb before him.

She peered at the object. It was hard to tell from a painting, but it appeared to have a slight sheen. Was it some sort of glass trinket handed down through the generations? Quite a lot of them had been holding it in varying degrees of firmness. Some with confidence, others with a springy hesitance as if it hurt. Perhaps something belonging to a distant past? Something *elven?*

Shaking her head, Alla plodded on. Anything of significance that the elven people might've had long ago would've been plucked from them by the neighbouring empire of Udynea, alongside the freedom of a great many refugees. At least, that's what she remembered from her mother. Odette and the other elves in the mansion knew nothing about their ancestors.

"Excuse me, my lady," called out a small, light voice. "Are you lost?"

Alla whirled on her heel to find a young human woman standing at the far end of the hall. Relief sagged her shoulders as she took in the pale blue palace livery. The servant seemed to be unaccompanied. "Terribly so," Alla replied, trotting towards the woman. "I was admiring the decor and seemed to have gotten turned around at some point. Could you perhaps show me the way back to the ballroom?"

The woman curtsied. "Certainly, my lady. This way." She turned, waiting for Alla to catch up before they left the hall with its array of orb-wielding portraits behind.

Chapter 8

The woman said nothing further whilst guiding Alla through the palace hallways. Alla had first mistaken the woman for a palace servant, but the golden stripe adorning the woman's downturned collar spoke differently. *A personal servant*. Perhaps one who worked directly for the royal family rather than someone who was merely employed by the royal estate or was assigned to a specific region of the palace. But certainly someone of greater status than the usual servant.

Halting before another entranceway also framed by light blue curtains, the woman gestured for Alla to continue without her. It wasn't the same entrance the others used. There were but the two of them.

Music—an ethereal harmony played by water magically driven through crystal tubes—drifted from the other side of the curtains, drawing Alla towards the entrance. She knew that tune. It was one her mother had hummed, some notes made possible only thanks to pure elven physiology. She hadn't expected to hear the same melody played within the palace. Certainly not for nobility.

Parting the curtain, Alla found herself on a narrow mezzanine overlooking the ballroom. *I made it*. She leant against the archway, her heart thumping wildly as she tried to take in everything at once lest it vanished before her eyes.

Cool, silvery-blue light bathed the room, the source a series of magical globes twirling near the ceiling, which was painted in a glorious vision of a desert coastline with camels running free across the crystal sands. The walls glittered beneath the glow, the silver sheen of the fractal reliefs in the carved panels lending an icy touch to the designs.

To her left, a grand stairway led down onto the dance floor. The crowd was a multitude of colours twisting and twirling as they mingled amongst each other, awaiting the arrival of the royal family. The current fashion was for big skirts, and she saw a fair number of them, but there were also plenty of women wearing the same slimmer style as herself. It eased the niggling worry of her standing out.

To her right, more people poured into the room from a less extravagant flight of steps. They paused at the top, spoke with a man, then waited as he announced them in a booming voice that seemed to ring from the very heavens.

Alla slunk along the wall, listening to the man. So far, none of the names he spoke were familiar. Her gaze slid across the crowd, searching for her stepmother or a hint of her stepsisters. She hadn't seen the carriage in the queue outside. Nor were they on the stairs, which meant they were already in the palace.

A row of archways, much like the one she had entered through, lined either side of the room. The ones opposite her led out into the night air. More curtains sectioned off the doorways, although many were tied back to frame each arch. Perhaps her stepmother was out there with Natalya. Her stepsister didn't do terribly well with crowds and this was the biggest grouping of people Alla had seen outside of the market.

But then why couldn't she spy Tamara? The woman was usually in the thick of any social gathering they attended. At least, according to Natalya's whining. Yet, Alla couldn't pick her from the crowd, either.

Pausing at the top of the grand stairs, Alla laid a hand on the thick pillar of the railing. Vines had entwined their way up and down the marble fluting. She brushed a fingertip against one of the small heart-shaped leaves. They were real and healthy, but she saw nowhere they could be potted.

"Presenting," the announcer boomed, "the Countess Antonia of—"

Gasping, Alla crouched behind the pillar before the man finished. She peeked around the belly of the column, peering through the vines, hoping the colour of her gown helped her blend in.

It was indeed her stepmother who stood at the top of the stairs whilst the announcer introduced Alla's stepsisters to the room.

Her stomach twisted. How long had the trio been standing there? *A while.* Several other people stood behind them with more lingering in the doorway. Had any of them spotted Alla?

No. Even if they had been looking for her, none of them could identify her at this distance. Not if she was barely able to make out their faces. At best, they would notice someone wearing a gown similar to something one of them owned. That wouldn't be a basis for suspicion.

Alla fiddled with her hair, pushing the hairpins deeper into her curls. *I can do this.* She just had to keep her distance and not do anything to draw attention to herself, then she would be gone by midnight and the three of them would be none the wiser.

"Are you hiding from anyone in particular?" The light voice was one she had heard before. Where? That was harder to place.

Refusing to abandon her crouch, Alla twisted around to look up into the brown eyes of a woman bedecked in a massive gown that was a crystalline shade of blue. Her skirts puffed out from her hips in a bloom of similar fabric, covered with a delicate layer of pearlescent silver lace. Flowers in pastel shades of pink, blue and yellow adorned the hem of the fabric.

All moisture fled Alla's mouth as her gaze ventured upwards, robbing her of speech. The top half of the woman's bodice was cut low in the modern fashion, a gauzy panel running down the front, exposing her breastbone. Unlike most of the dresses Alla had seen in the crowd, the gown had no sleeves or shoulders. Not that any delicate lace could possibly do justice to the woman's well-muscled frame. She wore gloves, though. Elbow-length and matching the pearlescent silver of the skirt lace.

Her long black hair was twisted into rope-like locs almost identical to the prince's hair—although the woman wore hers artfully draped over her shoulders whereas the prince had worn his tied back at the nape—they even had the same small clasps adorning them.

The woman beamed, seemingly oblivious to Alla's scrutiny. "Or are you merely hiding in general?"

"Hiding?" Alla managed before realising the inelegance of her position. She scrambled to her feet. With them both upright, the woman was still quite short in comparison to most humans. Still slightly taller than Alla—and that was including the small heels in her slippers aiding her stature by an inch.

"Was there someone you were trying to avoid?" The woman peered around Alla. "Forgive me for being forward, but you looked as though you'd seen the gaping maw of a hooded asp."

Alla shook her head. Being confronted by a hooded asp would be the least of her troubles. The most the snake could've done was kill her. Her stepmother could do a lot worse.

"No? Well then..." She spread her arms wide. "Allow me to welcome you to my ball."

"*Your*—?" *This* was the person the tsar was throwing the ball for? Not the prince?

Alla took in the light blue dress anew, along with the jewels glittering in the woman's hair. Added to the fact she was on this side of the room when everyone else was coming through the door or waiting below... It could only mean one thing. *Royalty.* Not the tsarina, but perhaps the prince's wife? *Although...* The woman looked familiar.

She tried to place the woman. The features were eerily similar to the prince. They had the same long face ending with a strong jaw, as well as sharply straight noses. Almost as if the two shared parentage. She'd only ever heard her stepsisters mention a Prince Viktor. Did they have it wrong? Did the tsar have two children?

Mentally shaking herself, Alla curtsied deeply. "Your highness, I am—"

The woman wrinkled her narrow nose. "Please, call me Viktoriya. Or Vik, if you'd like. My father does and I certainly would prefer it."

"Vik." The name fluttered up through her gut, dancing on her tongue. She crushed the sensation as swiftly as a butterfly beneath a cart wheel. If this was the prince's wife or betrothed, or even his sister, she would do better keeping her wits about her.

But her mind hissed and fizzed like chalk in scrubbing vinegar. It tumbled the name over in her head. Was the woman perhaps the prince's twin? It wasn't uncommon for them to be named similar, but that didn't negate not hearing her stepsisters mention a princess. Nor did it quash the nagging feeling that she had seen this woman before.

"And *you* are?" Princess Viktoriya prompted.

Heat flooded Alla's face. How long had she been staring at the woman? "I'm Alla," she mumbled. Should she inform the woman that the prince had invited her? Would she already know?

Princess Viktoriya's wide mouth parted with a grin that nearly split her face in two. "Lady Alla," she purred, seeming to savour the name. There was something about the lilt in her voice. A honeyed note.

Alla swallowed and ducked her head. Could the woman tell how her face was steadily becoming an inferno? Was she doing it deliberately?

The princess clasped Alla's hands. "It is nice to finally put a name to you."

Her brain at last caught up with her ears. In all her years, Alla had never met any two people who could sound so much alike. And she didn't speak mockingly, but sincere as though...

"Forgive me, your highness, but have we met?"

"We most certainly have," the princess insisted. "I might not remember everyone, but I would hardly forget someone so keen to avoid speaking with royalty that she practically raced her cart of goods out of the market."

"I don't see any situation in which I would've—" Market? *The invite.* But she hadn't met any princess. Unless...

She'd been wrong in having met the prince.

"*You*—" Alla curtsied low. *Twit.* She should've stuck with her first impression rather than let her stepsisters' nattering cloud her judgement. "Forgive my rudeness, your highness. I did not recognise you with your hair down and—"

"In a dress?" Princess Viktoriya supplied as Alla's voice faltered. She drew her hair back until it was largely bunched into one hand and free of her face. "Does this help?"

Heat, powerful enough to rival the sun, flooded Alla's cheeks until they tingled. She tried to mumble her agreement, but only a squeak escaped. The woman *had* been wearing a gorgeously fitted shirt and trousers the first time their paths had crossed, but how had she not noticed it sooner? "May I offer my most humblest of apologies? I did not realise it was *you* I spoke with that day." Her nerves, unable to be contained, bubbled out in a giggle. "I mistook you for the prince."

The princess' gentle smile fell.

"Not that I'm implying you and the prince look that much alike," Alla hastened to add, belatedly realising how her words could be misinterpreted. Her stepsisters hated being compared to each other, no matter their likeness. They could only have her beaten if they felt slighted, whereas royalty could do a lot worse.

Princess Viktoriya gave a dry chuckle. "I'd be surprised if I didn't bear a strong resemblance to the prince, given that we're one and the same. But if you still feel bad, you can make it up to me by being my first dance for the evening."

"I humbly beg your pardon, your highness. I must have misheard you." Whilst Alla doubted she had, she wasn't sure what the woman meant about her and the prince.

The princess opened her mouth. "I—"

"Presenting," the announcer boomed, stilling both chatter and music throughout the ballroom. "The debut of her regal highness and heir to the throne, Princess Viktoriya."

The woman grinned. "That's my cue." She strode out from behind the pillar to the top of the grand staircase where she gently waved and smiled to those below. "I am so very charmed to meet you all... again." The princess gave a deep laugh.

A few in the crowd followed suit.

Alla slunk back against the pillar, hoping to remain unseen as she watched the princess descend the stairs. *The heir?* That wasn't possible. Prince Viktor was their future ruler. Wasn't he? Inheritance went to the eldest living, regardless of gender.

Had something happened to the prince? Was that why the tsar had the ball, to let the empire's nobility greet the woman who would be their new ruler? Her stepsisters likely hadn't understood the crier or only glanced at whatever letters they received. *I should've listened properly in the market.* That would've kept her from embarrassing herself and clearly making the princess feel uncomfortable.

"The princess shall now choose a partner for the first dance."

A fair number of the people in the crowd, both men and women, adjusted garments or attempted to sidle closer to the princess, especially those standing closest to the grand stairs.

Princess Viktoriya seemed intent on ignoring them all. Turning ever-so-slightly, she motioned for Alla to come down.

Disbelief and alarm froze her limbs before reason regained control. Shaking her head, Alla abandoned the pillar to slink further back from the stairs until she was hidden in the shadows of a curtain. *I shouldn't have come.* But who could've predicted the princess would even speak to her, let alone ask for a dance?

Seemingly undeterred, Princess Viktoriya trotted back up the stairs to the shocked murmurs of the crowd. She lingered by the curtain, drawing it back just enough for Alla to see her face. "I'm uncertain if you realised it, but that was *your* cue."

Alla shuffled her feet. "I realised, but I really shouldn't." To risk having her stepmother pick her out from the crowd was one thing, to be the focus of everyone as she danced with the princess? Unthinkable.

Tilting her head up, the princess eyed Alla with a haughty expression that was somewhat dulled by the gleam of humour creasing her eyes. "Are you refusing a royal request, my lady?"

"Of course not." She had tried that already with the invitation, which hadn't gone well. "I just..." She glanced at the crowd, barely visible through the railing. Her stepmother stood at the foot of the stairs opposite them. As long as they remained a fair distance from the trio, they wouldn't be able to easily place her. "I've never danced in public."

"But you know how?" She took Alla's hand and gently guided her to the top of the stairs before Alla could do more than nod. "Follow my lead and you'll do fine."

Chapter 9

Music started playing as Alla followed the princess down the grand staircase. The notes drifted through the air like clouds, buoying her even as her shoes clacked at every other step. She didn't know how possible dancing in them would be, but with the gentle melody whispering in her ears, she was prepared to try.

The crowd nearest the stairs withdrew as Princess Viktoriya reached the bottom. Such migratory movements left a wide space before the stairs, more than enough for a couple to comfortably dance.

Led by Princess Viktoriya's gentle tug, Alla swung around, standing before the woman. It meant her back was to the crowd, but having her face hidden could only be a good thing. Seemingly unsatisfied with the position, the princess coaxed Alla closer.

Thankfully, Uda hadn't settled on one of her stepsister's fuller gowns. The lack of layers enabled Alla to follow the princess' subtle directions without worry about the abundance of petticoats between them. Even now, she wasn't certain that taking another step closer to the princess was an option.

It could've been Alla's imagination, but there seemed to be a nervous waver stretching Princess Viktoriya's lips and tightening her eyes as the princess placed her hands upon Alla's waist. They swayed from side to side as the music continued its dreamy melody. The movement did little to affect Alla's dress, but the princess' blue dress looked as though the flowing and floating skirts were woven from the very heavens by divine hands.

Every inch the princess. Just as she'd been in the marketplace.

Alla's face heated. She had been right and wrong at the same time, a somewhat jarring sensation. "I feel so foolish for not sticking with my initial feeling that you were a woman when we first met." She had only considered the option after being informed that the person she spoke with was royalty, with the additional knowledge of the tsar having but one child. Information she had overheard from her stepsisters. *I should've known better.* Served her right for not verifying such facts herself. "I truly cannot apologise enough for that, your highness."

Princess Viktoriya smiled, the tip of her nose twitching ever so slightly. "The misunderstanding as to the nature of my title is barely a flutter against the worst retorts I've experienced, especially given that we had just met. And I'm sure it'll be a running theme for tonight." Her lashes closed until only a thin gleam of reflected light glittered between them. "But I shall take your appearance here and this dance as recompense."

The gentle strum of a stringed instrument—an elven lap harp, judging by the crystal clink at the end of each note—shimmered through the otherwise lulling notes.

Without thinking, Alla took up the princess' hands, cradling the slim fingers. *So smooth.* Not that she had expected it any other way, but she couldn't remember clasping a hand that wasn't scarred or marked by hours of work. Did the woman feel the difference? Would she wonder why a noble had the coarse and calloused hands of a labourer?

Princess Viktoriya's brow twitched. If she *had* noticed, she chose not to breathe a word, merely taking a firmer hold of Alla's fingers and leading them through the first few steps as they danced in small circles across the floor. They shuffled back and forth to the lap harp's slow strums, always keeping that little bit to each other's left.

Their easy steps enabled Alla to keep her feet comparatively close to the floor, enough to reduce any clacking from her borrowed shoes. Even when they swung closer to the edge of the crowd, she suffered no unexpected slippage from the footwear. Although, she had yet to perspire and dreaded how well the ill-fitting shoes would remain in place.

Murmurs drifted alongside the music, although the snippets of conversation made a nonsensical jumble as they twirled by. So many brief murmurs and whispered words.

"...I never..."

"...you imagine?"

"...wouldn't..."

Alla nevertheless knew what, and who, their talk centred on. "Everyone's talking about us." Their white-hot stares prickled up her spine, reminding her that her stepmother and stepsisters were out there. How close had Princess Viktoriya brought them to the entrance stairs? Did the trio still linger there? Had Alla been spotted? She couldn't pick them out from the other blurred faces in the crowd.

"Of course they're talking about us," the princess agreed as they circled each other, the back of one hand resting in the small of her back. "What better fodder for their gossip than their beloved heir plucking a woman from atop the grand stairs rather within than the crowd? And all whilst flouncing around in a dress."

Alla tilted her head, trying to focus on the conversation even as she searched for her stepmother. She thought she had perhaps misheard earlier, but there was no mistaking what the princess had said. "You're really the heir to the throne?"

Princess Viktoriya hummed her agreement. She swung around to face Alla and guided them through a few more intricate sweeps of the available space.

The rest of the crowd slowly faded away as Alla allowed herself to be led, vaguely aware they were returning to the foot of the grand staircase. The music would stop soon. As would this floating sensation deep within her.

Yet, a small nagging question refused to let her be carried away on the melody. "I thought the title of heir went to Prince Viktor. Is he not the eldest?" She had thought herself only misinformed on the number of children the tsar had sired, not the order of their births.

"Eldest?" the princess echoed, laughing. The deep, shoulder-shaking sound had the surrounding nobility chattering avidly amongst themselves. "I was trying to explain it earlier, but rest assured my parents have just the one child." She delicately laid her free hand upon her chest. "That would be me."

Alla halted, and was dragged a stumbling step forward as the princess failed to stop quite as swiftly. Her foot slipped alarmingly within the shoe's confines, threatening to twist her ankle. She hastened to right herself before she lost either shoes or her balance.

Thankfully, the princess was quick to assist her. "Are you all right?" There was a whisper of disappointment within the words, an old weariness that fought its confinement which Alla doubted had anything to do with the state of her wellbeing.

"Yes, thank you. I—" Alla fussed with her hair, ensuring her ears were still covered. "That wasn't quite the answer I expected, is all." It made a lot more sense.

Presenting her royal highness. A debut fit for a princess, but only because she had been forced to be the prince for... How long?

Her fingertip brushed the point of her ear through the strands. She was hiding the real her, even if only for a little while, because it was easier. Was that not similar to having everyone believe a lie crafted by others? It seemed to her that the only difference was how the princess could reveal her true self to the world without fear.

Princess Viktoriya stood still, her hands clasped before her. No less patient than before, but she suddenly seemed exhausted. Her face drawn.

"You are a woman." Alla stepped closer, her skirts pressing against the great swaths of blue silk and lace. "But they believed otherwise?" There was only one reason they'd come to that conclusion.

The princess gave a curt nod, her brow furrowing.

"Wasn't it obvious?" Had she been misgendered at birth? How many years had the woman been forced to live another life? Surely, no one person could pretend to be two people for long without suffering some sort of mental harm.

Princess Viktoriya's gaze lifted. She flashed a smug smile. "I've always thought so. It took my parents a while to come around to the notion."

"And now the world sees the real you. Not the... other one."

The princess looked down at herself. "I've always been me.

But I guess you're right. Everyone now knows their beloved Prince Viktor wasn't the true reflection of myself." She shrugged. "That's what this ball is about, showing off the real me to the court."

"It must've been terribly draining." Alla found it difficult to maintain her usual facade of being only human whilst at the market. And that was only once a month. She couldn't imagine having to do it for days—weeks, months, *years*—on end.

Like a parting fog, a sliver of weariness faded from the woman's face even as that same emotion lifted her shoulders. "It's getting better." She glanced around, startled, as if only now becoming aware they had stopped dancing. Even the music had ended. "I suppose..." She spread her skirts wide and dipped a minuscule curtsy.

Alla replied in kind, albeit a lot deeper.

The crowd politely clapped. Some leant towards another, gossiping away in their companion's ear. None could've heard Alla's conversation with the princess, although many in the crowd likely wondered at the cause behind the sudden cessation of their dancing.

She swung back to face the princess. "No one really calls you *Vik*, do they?"

"They have done, although not for some time. A shame as I quite prefer it. I chose the name, after all."

"You chose Viktor?" It wasn't uncommon for royalty to have three or more alterations to their name as they grew up and suited another better. Other nobles occasionally followed suit—although if her stepsisters could be believed, the trend was dying out—but no one had ever spoken of the children choosing their new names.

The princess shook her head. "It was always Viktoriya. There was my first name, obviously, but the rest came after what I had chosen. The first syllable slipped through my mother's lips and, rather than out me at the tender age of ten to a few members of the court before I was ready for the world to know, she left it at the brief explanation of me already suiting another name." Her lips twisted sourly for a brief moment. "Rumour decided that her fond moniker of Vik must be short for Viktor."

Alla nodded her understanding. No doubt, there had been no

movement to alter that rumour or its spread. "And now the court knows the truth."

Princess Viktoriya squared her shoulders and gave a curt nod. "I'm sure my mother's preference to call me Viky will also ram that home. Although, I do find it a little twee. Don't you agree?"

A tinkling harmony of strings and flutes started playing before Alla could think of a reply. *The next dance.* Whilst she had never been to a ball, she knew the formalities when it came to young, unwed nobles. "I suppose I should let you get on with choosing another dance partner." Alla dipped slightly in farewell as she took a step back.

"I *should* be choosing another, yes," Princess Viktoriya murmured, her gaze drifting over the expectant crowd. Her lips curled for a brief moment before flattening. "On the other hand, why dither about in exploring other options when perfection has already been crafted? If you would..." She held out her hand. "A second dance, Lady Alla?"

Alla glanced back at the entrance stairs, the fresh bustle of the crowd exposing its whole length. Her stepmother had indeed vanished from sight. Where to? *Somewhere within the crowd.* She couldn't begin to fathom how she would pick any of the trio from the twirling mass of flesh and fabric.

There. Not on the stairway, but near it. Her focus seemed to be on something in the opposite direction, quite possibly one of her daughters. If that were true, then she wouldn't be concerned with searching for a familiar face that she believed had no right to be here, especially if Alla managed to keep her distance.

She clasped the princess' offered hand and curtsied low. "I would love another dance, your highness."

Others in the crowd also started dancing. They twirled along to the music in dainty circles, skirts flaring at the power of each twirl. Alla followed, albeit at a pace that wouldn't send her shoes flying.

The crowd's whirling moves swiftly encroached on their space. Several of the dancers bumped into them. Enough to be dismissed as a mere accident, but it set Alla's heart to racing all the same. It wouldn't take much to upset her balance and send her toppling to the floor where her ears could risk being exposed.

After the fifth such instance, Princess Viktoriya gave an exasperated huff and stopped all attempts at navigating their dance steps to avoid the crowd. "Come." With a gentle tug on Alla's hand, she made for the grand staircase. "Let us go where there's a little more room."

She followed the princess without question. Being further from the dancers also reduced her chance of being identified by her stepsisters, who were likely engaged in wooing whatever nobleman had chosen them for a dance partner.

They reached the top of the landing with little trouble and, away from those cavorting below, resumed their dance.

Alla attempted to keep up with the quick movements, but after their previous dancing, the shoes had become hard and unforgiving. And, whenever she dared a proper step, she got the uncertain feeling of walking on a waxed tile in stockings.

By the third misstep, it felt as though her feet were no longer hers to control.

"Sorry," she gabbled. "I didn't have any shoes that fitted." She didn't have any at all, but she was able to restrain her tongue enough to keep that information to herself. "So I... kind of... borrowed these from my half-sister. Along with the dress." Appalled by her own lack of restraint, she bit her tongue lest anything else slipped free.

Princess Viktoriya gave a small, sympathetic smile. "You know what? I'm finding my own footwear a little cumbersome. Shall we dispense with them?" The princess was already kicking off her shoes before Alla could respond. Much to Alla's dismay, the woman's height didn't diminish by a drastic amount.

Alla followed suit, grumbling slightly under her breath at losing the inch difference in height as she slipped off her borrowed shoes and placed them near the wall. The tiles beneath her feet were cool and smooth, much like the foyer back home. She had done a little bit of dancing on such a surface, during the good days when her stepmother seemed to forget she existed.

Barefoot once more, her balance and grace returned. It allowed her to glide along the landing. Princess Viktoriya must've noticed Alla's regained confidence, for she increased the pace to match the music's beat and the other dancers' movements.

They twirled around the landing in silence. The silvery-blue light shimmered along Princess Viktoriya's gown with every swish and glittered amongst the small clasps adorning her locs.

One such movement had their figures twirling out from each other to face the crowd below. The princess snickered, her gaze fastened on the dance floor where couples twirled in similar steps. "Just look at how they circle the ballroom." She jerked her chin at the uncoupled nobles impatiently waiting on the sidelines for their chance to join in. "Like wild dogs hunting for scraps."

"But you're not a piece of meat." Alla idly swept her gaze across the rest of the room before slipping from the woman's grasp and diving behind the pillar. She spied Tamara dancing with a red-headed man way on the other side of the ballroom. She also swore there was a flash of her other stepsister standing nearby. But her stepmother? The woman was nowhere to be seen.

Princess Viktoriya carried on dancing for a few steps before realising Alla hadn't followed. "Alla? Are you all right?"

Had she been spotted? *Of course, you fool.* She wouldn't expect anyone to ignore the princess dancing with someone, especially when that chosen partner was an unknown woman. But had any of them identified her?

Clasping Alla's shoulders, Princess Viktoriya neatly slipped between her and the crowd. "Clearly, there's someone you're trying to avoid. Who?"

Alla shook her head. If she revealed too much, then this magical evening could become her last. She would do better to leave any reasoning of who and why to the princess' imagination, but she really needed to—

"Go," Alla blurted. "I should..." Whether she had been recognised or not, making herself scarce was the best option. "Get away from all this."

Princess Viktoriya smiled and gently cupped Alla's elbow, guiding her to their footwear. "Then, come with me. I know just the place."

Chapter 10

Alla remained silent, unsure of their destination, as the princess escorted her through the blue curtains and down the same corridors she had previously walked with the palace servant. The princess was far better company, walking at her side with their fingers linked.

Alla's shoes dangled in her free hand, enabling her to enjoy the rich sensation of the carpet upon her soles. She had thought use would've robbed the threads of their plushness, just as what had happened at home, but she was able to dig her toes into the pile at every languid step. It was like walking on moss.

The walls of the corridors opened out into the hall dotted with portraits.

Even here, with its cool air and the abundance of seating before each painting, Princess Viktoriya showed no hint of stopping. But there was an absence of urgency in their passage.

Alla's stomach knotted as they strolled down the middle of the room. She glanced at the portraits, trying not to see the poorly hidden elven qualities. One thing she did notice was that a lot of the portraits had one of the couple wearing a key. Sometimes, it was the tsar, other times, the tsarina, always peeking out from within their jewels.

Princess Viktoriya wore the same key around her neck or at least a replica. She toyed with it as they walked, delicately twirling the shaft between her thumb and forefinger.

"So..." Alla drawled, trying to fill what had been comfortable silence before they had entered the hall. "If I have this right, your parents threw a massive ball, inviting all of the nobility, because they've accepted you are a woman?"

The princess' lips flattened. "Not entirely, but close enough. They accepted the fact years ago, but my father has worried himself sick about the court's reaction and my safety amongst them. Needlessly, it would seem."

"I would've thought they'd insist on having your heir coronation some time ago." Alla surreptitiously eyed the princess. She looked older than the usual eighteen-year-old human.

Princess Viktoriya nodded. "My first appearance as a prince and their future tsar was done when I was twelve. So yes, I guess thirteen years ago is a while back."

Peering off into the distance, vaguely aware they were leaving the hall for another corridor, Alla's thoughts crackled and buzzed with questions. The heir coronation was always performed before the court, so they would know who was next in line. "Then, I'm afraid I don't understand the need for another debut? Aren't you the same person?"

"I've asked myself that very question." She shrugged. "*I* could've done without the ball, but my mother was adamant I get an introduction as befits a princess, rather than some dry announcement. She says it's more fitting. Although, I've never been all that good at the whole court mingling side of things."

Alla thought of the way the princess had floated around the ballroom, of her strength and poise then and even now. "One would be hard-pressed to realise that. You've done a marvellous job of it tonight."

Surprise flickered across the princess' face and fluttered her lashes. "Oh? Thank you. Although, I must confess, everything surrounding tonight was my mother's choice. The music, the dancing..." She ran a hand down the gown's bodice. "The dress."

"Well, she has excellent tastes. And she must be a loving person to accept you as you truly are." Alla couldn't imagine her stepmother allowing any such liberties.

They stepped through an archway curving along a path in a small garden. Moon ivy ran up the pillars, their pale blossoms almost glowing in the meagre lantern light. She slipped her hand free of the princess' grasp to cup one of the flowers, its delicate petals slightly fuzzy.

The princess settled on a bench backed by a bush with fan-shaped leaves. "Come, please." She patted the bench's stone seat. "Sit." The woman's dark eyes seemed to glow with light, a trait Alla saw more in elves than humans. No doubt, a residual trait from the unspoken elven ancestry. Did it mean she also saw the same as Alla in this low light? Of how the hedges sheltered the garden and lent an air of seclusion to the almost intimate space.

Alla settled on the bench, her back to the lantern.

"Truthfully," the princess whispered, drawing closer as if divulging a great secret. "There was another aspect to this night that wasn't announced. My father wanted me to wait until I had found a wife to bear my children, but my mother saw this as an opportunity to see what fish are willing to bite now that I am of marriageable age."

Alla's heart sank at the bitterness in Princess Viktoriya's words. If her stepmother knew the truth behind tonight, the woman would stop at nothing to see one of her daughters was chosen. It wouldn't matter to her that neither Tamara nor Natalya liked women in that fashion. "Poor Vik," she murmured.

Princess Viktoriya hummed her agreement, her lips flattening into a thin line. "Mother thought it better I face the whole court as the princess I am rather than the prince they thought they had. At once." She shook her head. "They still insist I marry a woman. Because, you know, carrying a child is something I can't do myself." Her tone seemed cheerful and flippant enough, but the smile she gave Alla didn't quite reach her eyes.

Alla had never given any thought to having children—at least, not beyond what her stepmother might do to them if she did. And when the only option to her was to proposition a serf or servant? It certainly wasn't happening.

She gently laid her hand upon Princess Viktoriya's knee. "I'm sorry. Truly. I've never considered how hard it must be to know the future of a whole lineage rests on you."

"Do your shoulders not bear the same weight?"

Alla shook her head. "My lineage is nothing in comparison."

Or at all. So few of noble breeding would look to muddy their line by introducing elven blood into it.

Princess Viktoriya patted Alla's fingers and flicked her hair over her shoulder. "Truthfully, I don't mind the marrying part. Just because I am a woman doesn't mean I don't find my own gender attractive." She leant back, resting her hands behind her to keep from falling off the bench. "You understand?"

With her face heating, Alla tucked her hair behind her ear. She did indeed. Quite a bit.

Princess Viktoriya's brows lowered, along with the gentle curve of her lips. She reached out, her gloved hand brushing against Alla's ear.

Terror clutched her heart, even as a pleasing jolt from the contact bubbled in her gut. How had she become so at ease around the princess to forget the need to hide her ears? *Stupid girl.*

"Oh, Alla..." she breathed. "You needn't look so frightful. I—" She fell silent as her gaze fell on Alla's mouth. "I have no intention of harming you. I swear. I would be the last person to even think of it."

Alla wasn't sure when, but at some point, their hands had found one another. Rather than extract her fingers from the princess' grasp, she wet her lips and tried not to think about how Princess Viktoriya mimicked the gesture or that their faces were only inches apart. *Almost close enough to kiss.*

A flush of heat suffused her cheeks as the thought—the highly inappropriate thought—fluttered through her mind. Brief, at first, then with a persistence that set her heart to hammering and her breath rasping like a wood saw. All she could think of was how closely the princess sat, how her lips glistened in the moonlight, how soft they looked, how brazen she would have to be to dare a taste...

She leant forward, before logic and fear could take hold, and pressed her lips to the princess'.

Princess Viktoriya's mouth parted a little, a gasp of surprise filling the space. Before Alla could consider withdrawing, the princess was kissing back. She pulled Alla close. One gloved hand snaked around her waist, whilst the other cupped her jaw.

Alla closed her eyes, taking in the softness and sweetness

with which the princess returned the kiss. Her heart pounded with the firmness of her grasp. Strong. Intoxicating.

Princess Viktoriya's hand moved up, a thumb caressing the underside of Alla's ear as the woman's fingers ran through her hair. A muffled groan tightened Alla's throat. Did the princess know how sensitive they were, of the heat each brush evoked through Alla? She certainly didn't seem of a mind to stop.

Alla's own touch wandered up the princess' arms, curling her fingers around those bare shoulders.

The dull clack of footsteps echoed from the path.

Stiffening, Princess Viktoriya drew back. She slowly adjusted Alla's hair before she stood, putting herself between whoever was approaching and Alla.

A woman trotted through the archway. "Viky, dear, there you are." She strode along the path, her skirts billowing behind her like a pennant.

Then the sight was lost to Alla's limited viewpoint as the princess tucked her further behind.

"Now, I know you're only indulging me with this ball," the woman continued, seemingly oblivious. "But that doesn't mean you can vanish whenever you—" The woman halted as Princess Viktoriya stepped to one side. "Oh! I had no idea you were entertaining someone." The woman's gaze alighted on Alla. "Hello?"

"Mother," Princess Viktoriya said, angling herself so that she remained between them. She flashed Alla a reassuring smile. "May I introduce Lady Alla?"

Alla leapt to her feet and curtsied deeply, her heart thundering harder than a bolting horse. The bareness of her feet loomed in her mind. Hopefully, her skirts hid her feet and how her shoes sat under the bench. "Your imperial majesty," she gabbled. "Forgive me for not recognising you sooner. The light—"

The tsarina waved aside Alla's attempt at explaining, then clasped Alla's hand in both of hers. "I don't believe I've seen you in court."

"Your majesty is correct. I haven't been able to make it to the palace before tonight." Whilst not precisely a lie, the slight omission did twist her stomach.

Princess Viktoriya cleared her throat, quietly slipping

further between them until the tsarina had no choice but to relinquish her hold. "Lady Alla spends much of her time assisting with the running of her family estate. And…" Her gaze flicked to Alla. "…charity works with the poor."

"A most noble calling and a product of many interesting tales, I am sure." The tsarina exchanged a meaningful look with her daughter. They held each other's gaze before the woman smiled softly. "I shall take my leave and inform the Ghosts of your whereabouts."

Ghosts? Alla knew of only one type that the tsarina could summon: Those who were born from magical bloodlines but lacked the gift of conjuring or the ability to be directly affected by magic.

"It was a pleasure to meet you, my dear," said the tsarina.

Realising the woman spoke to her, Alla bobbed her deepest curtsy. "And you, your imperial majesty."

The tsarina bowed her head in acknowledgement and departed, albeit, a lot slower and with quite a few glances over her shoulder until she disappeared beneath the archway.

Issuing a groan, Princess Viktoriya collapsed back onto the bench. "That's all I need, Ghosts following me like a bad smell."

"Your mother sent them to watch us? Was it me?" She turned to the princess. "I hope I didn't offend her."

"It's all right," Princess Viktoriya said, her hands raised placatingly before her. "They are sent wherever I am, regardless of my company. You needn't be alarmed by their presence." She flashed a cheeky grin. "Unless, of course, you actually mean me harm."

"*Never*, your highness."

"*Vik*."

Inclining her head, Alla repeated the princess' name. It still brought an airy flutter to her gut. "I've never met a Ghost." Most were either born into the families they protected or bought as infants for a lord's ransom. The first method was rare. Her household wasn't influential enough to bother with the second.

"You could have whilst being entirely unawares. They look no different from other people." Princess Viktoriya swung her feet as she gave a thoughtful hum. "Do you recall Ivan? The man I was travelling with?"

Alla shook her head. She remembered bumping into a guard whilst retrieving her wares, but not much after the princess had made her presence known. Certainly not anyone else's name.

"Oh." Disappointed, the princess' bottom lip twitched into a pout. "Well, he is one of my personal Ghosts. And rather... *dutiful*." She sneered as the word flew from her mouth. "I daresay he'll be the one mother sends to look over us."

"If I may ask?" Alla waited for the woman's swift nod before continuing. "What did you mean when you told the tsarina I assist in running my family's estate?" How did the princess know more about her than Alla had revealed? Had her stepmother somehow warned the woman? Was that why they had left the ballroom far behind? Was she being set up?

Leaning forward, her shoulders bunched as her palms pressed against the bench. Princess Viktoriya eyed her. "That *was* what you were doing when I met you in the marketplace, wasn't it?"

Alla hummed thoughtfully. She supposed it was one way to spin procuring the estate's monthly wares. "And the charity part?" She helped those she met during her travels when and where she could, but Princess Viktoriya couldn't possibly know that.

"The young elven girl sitting atop your cart? I assume she wasn't beholden to you beforehand. She looked to be in a dreadful state, yet you don't strike me as the type who would let things get that far."

That was true, but far more importantly... "She isn't beholden to me, then or now." The last thing she would ever seek from another being was serfdom or any form of enslavement. "Mady isn't in a fit state to work in any capacity." Alla hated to think what would've become of the girl had those enslavers caught her. *Nothing good.* She had heard whispers of there being worse places to be sold to than one of the glass barons. She dreaded the idea of what they could be. "But when she is, she will remain a free being."

Princess Viktoriya's brows rose. "That's quite the modern outlook."

A thin spark of pride had her bristling at the words. "My father—"

The princess held up her hand. "I mean no disrespect. It's just... I've been trying to get *my* father to see a path beyond the *traditional*—" Her lips twisted in distaste. "—for so long." She spread her arms wide. "Look at what we have. How can we call ourselves civilised and better than the neighbouring empires when the same problems gnaw at our roots? Serfdom. Such an innocuous word. Used to hide the same nastiness. Would it not be better for all of Niholia's people if they weren't shackled into such a broken system?"

"That was what my father believed." He had always insisted that people did their best when working to better their own lives and that *his* job as a noble and a landowner was to ensure those relying on him had a safe and stable place to do so. And to do it secure in the knowledge that they could leave whenever they chose.

"Believed?" Princess Viktoriya said, her expression suddenly stiff. "*Was?* Did he change his mind or...?"

"He passed away some years ago." Over a decade, in fact. She'd only been ten years of age. "There was a battle at the northern border. He had volunteered months prior. *'To help push back the Obuzan force'* as he would say." Her father's retinue had been instrumental in winning the battle that had taken his life, although the war continued to this day. "He—" She all but choked on the word. Wetness trickled down her cheek, turning chill in the gentle breeze.

Slowly, Princess Viktoriya knelt before Alla. She laid her hand upon Alla's cheek and softly wiped away the tears with the brush of her thumb. "I am so sorry."

Alla grimaced. "I should be the one apologising." She hastily dried her face, rubbing viciously at her cheeks. "I'm not usually this... awkward." Put her in the fields, or the middle of a kitchen, and she knew precisely what to do. But the genteel arts of the court? They eluded her.

Was her stepmother right? Did her common blood—her elven parentage—make her unsuitable for the court? Her father had never thought so, not even of her mother.

The princess chuckled. "Well, I know something about feeling out of your depth." She cleared her throat, all signs of jest wiped from her face. Her dark gaze settled on Alla. "I had no idea of the risks you took in coming here. I feel so selfish for having insisted. Had I but known..."

"*I* knew, though." There wasn't a day that went by where her stepmother didn't make Alla's tenuous position in the mansion blatantly obvious. "I still chose to come."

"And I'm very glad you did. But I'm surprised you don't appear to be even the teeniest bit scared. Most elves I meet are appallingly timid."

"I am *half* elven." A strange pressure lifted from around her chest as she spoke. "And there's little you could do to me that my stepmother hasn't done or threatened." From slavery to death, her stepmother had wielded them all above her head at one time or the other. Only the former threat still had teeth as Alla grew older and realised death would be a momentary concern.

A strange, slightly unnerving, gleam entered Princess Viktoriya's eyes. "She has?" Plucking up Alla's shoes, she gestured to an archway crafted from the hedge. "How about you tell me more whilst we walk?"

Chapter 11

Alla chatted at great length about her stepmother, starting all the way back to when the woman and her daughters first entered Alla's life and continuing through each and every punishment her stepmother had doled out. The lies, the threats, the beatings. The derogation and outright ignoring of her title and place in the mansion.

Princess Viktoriya remained silent through all of it, not even issuing the customary sympathetic hum Alla had garnered from others as a child. Her expression was a different matter. She winced at each mention of physical force, grimaced at the threats and lies, and pursed her lips whenever Alla mentioned her father.

Only when Alla reached the conclusion of her tale— of the rage her stepmother had flown into that had led to Alla's secret journey to the ball via the cart—did a solemn sigh gust from the princess' lips. "To be subjected to one such transgression would be horrid enough. I am sorry you were put through so many."

"Why? You've had no hand in it." She smiled, hoping to ease the princess' mind, although it seemed to have little effect. "It's not so bad. Others have to deal with far worse than I." Whilst she was treated no better than the mansion's serfs, she wasn't truly one of them. And she had a roof over her head. Many of those with elven heritage had nothing. Most were worked to death by the glass barons.

"*That*," Princess Viktoriya murmured, "Sounds like an

excuse for her behaviour. Suffering is not a contest. What wounds one can kill another."

Alla knew the truth of those words all too well. "What else could I have done? It was my father's estate, my home. If I had inherited it, I would've thrown her out in a heartbeat, but I was born of an elven woman and half-breeds don't get the same privileges as their human parent."

She sometimes wondered what her father would've done had he known the truth. Would he have persisted in choosing love over custom? Would he have raised her with all these ideals that the world told her was wrong?

The princess hummed thoughtfully. "Did *she* tell you that?"

Nodding wearily, Alla turned her attention to their surroundings. She couldn't recall how long, or how far, they had walked through the gardens, only that everything was so lushly green. She hadn't seen the like since the date trees died.

They had left the hedge-bordered alcoves and carefully shaped foliage far behind before Alla had gotten to her first mention of a lashing; given at eleven years of age. Her gaze alighted on the bush beside them.

Everything around them seemed a touch untamed and exotic. The bulk of the bush before her consisted of great purple and deep blue fan-shaped flowers that her mother had called Night Wings. Memory told her it was quite water-hungry. "It must take a lot out of your gardeners to keep all this healthy." She peered through the foliage. "I see signs of irrigation but no source."

"That would be the oasis. It feeds off an underground spring and the irrigation system is funnelled from the same source. In fact, all the palace water comes from there."

"Oasis?"

Princess Viktoriya motioned for her to step around a particularly leafy bush that separated their path back to the palace and follow her deeper into the undergrowth.

Alla had expected to find a pond, maybe slightly larger than the one on her family's estate. Or perhaps an artificial pool sectioned off by carved stone as had been depicted in several of the paintings adorning the foyer.

The reflective body of water was almost a lake. This far from the palace, the only light was that of a half moon, but it was more than enough to see by. Palms, reeds, rushes and ferns ringed the area whilst lily pads as big around as a bed floated upon the water's surface. Small birds wandered the area, no doubt disturbed by their presence.

"You have herons?" Blue ones at that. They were supposed to bring luck and good fortune to the land they chose as their roost. The ones back home had fled with the dying date trees.

Princess Viktoriya hummed her agreement, her mind clearly elsewhere. "I wonder... if you will indulge my curiosity?"

"Most definitely." It was the least she could do after bending the woman's ear with her troubles. And for who knew how long?

They found a slab of stone near the water big enough to sit upon, even with it half-crowded by a leafy bush and nestled under the bowing branches of a tree Alla couldn't identify. The tree leaves hung in long tendrils, hovering just above the water's surface. Alla set her shoes near the stone's base.

Perched on the edge of the stone, Princess Viktoriya twisted to face her. "Your parents were married before your birth? And you say your father owned the estate before he married your stepmother?"

A wary tingle ran up Alla's spine as she bobbed her head in a quick nod. It had belonged to his family line for multiple generations. Maybe even as far back as before the elven arrival to the continent or the forming of Niholia.

"And your father had no other children?"

"Not that I'm aware of." If there were any, they certainly didn't know her father was dead or they would've contested her stepmother's ownership of the estate.

"Then you are his heir. The ownership passes to the eldest child. Everything he owned is yours, the estate included. Granted, you were a child at the time, but your stepmother could only become your regent."

Laughter bubbled out Alla's mouth before she could contain her mirth. "Me? Inherit?" True, she'd been too young to run an estate when her father died and her stepmother had taken over, but she'd never thought she could inherit everything her father owned. Why would she?

"Didn't you know?"

Alla shook her head and toyed with a half-closed bud of a

flower on the bush. No one had told her anything about inheritance since her mother's death. That a wife would get first bite was an easy and logical assumption to reach as any other.

Princess Viktoriya hummed and mumbled just under her breath, then said, "Regency, when you were so young, would be easy to claim, but you are surely old enough to take command over what is yours."

"Who would stand by me?" Her stepmother had done more than merely mind the estate whilst Alla grew up. "She traded most of the estate's serfs." Although, if what the princess said was true, Alla supposed they had technically belonged to her. *Including Uda and Odette.* She wasn't certain how she felt about that. Beyond queasy. "She fired the servants and brought in fresh serfs to replace them. Her efforts have run our little farm into the ground."

"The deeds will state—"

"If there are still deeds to that land, then she has them tucked away where I would never find them." If her stepmother hadn't burnt them long ago. Was she the type to risk losing everything to keep Alla from her birthright? All because she was a half-breed and, in her stepmother's eyes, unworthy of her status?

What if the taxes paid weren't enough? They could swipe the house right out from under everyone. All because of some jealous, petty—

Alla grasped the flower's stem, prepared to tear it from the bush. Pain lanced through her finger. She jerked her hand back, instinctively putting the wounded digit in her mouth. The tang of blood hit her tongue. She hadn't noticed the plant having thorns.

"Here." Princess Viktoriya held out her hand. "Let me fix it for you."

Alla shook her head. It was only a scratch, nothing immediately life-threatening. "I'm fine. I—" Her tongue stilled as the princess laid a hand on her shoulder. A tingle slithered through her, there for a breath and then gone, along with the pain in her finger.

"See? That barely took any..." The princess' gaze lifted, settling just below the collar of Alla's dress. "...time?" She raised a hand, delicately sliding it around to the nape of Alla's neck and retrieving the chain from its confines beneath the gown. "You are contained?" Princess Viktoriya caressed the necklace, her expression blank. "Amazing. I thought *infitialis* dulled the senses, but you..." She smiled warmly. "If you are this compassionate whilst wearing that, then I would love to know you without it." Her lashes lowered part way, her eyes dark without the moonlight gleaming in them. "To kiss you with nothing dulling your full passion."

Alla ducked her head, her cheeks growing hotter the longer the woman talked. She had lived with the chain for so long that she'd forgotten what it was like to be without it. The memory used to be there, a shadow of how vibrant the world had been, but now? It slipped from her thoughts like a noonday dream.

"I can have it removed," Princess Viktoriya offered, the back of her finger caressing Alla's neck, sending a fresh surge of warmth through her veins. "My Ghosts are able." She twisted as if there was someone capable of the task nearby.

Alla shook her head. There was no telling what her stepmother would do if she returned to the mansion without the chain. And she would need to do so soon if she was to meet up with Odette and Uda. She wasn't even sure how far her stroll with the princess had taken her, for the palace seemed quite small in the moonlight. *The moon.* It was quite high. Her chest tightened, panic squeezing her heart. "It's almost midnight."

Princess Viktoriya glanced up at the sky. "Very nearly."

"It isn't—" She hopped to her feet. "I thought..." Bobbing a sloppy curtsy, she ducked, groping in her own shadow for her borrowed shoes. "Forgive me. I didn't realise it was so late. I really must go. Thank you for such a wonderful night. I'll never forget it." Shoes found, she flashed the princess a warm smile.

"Go where? Back to that thing you say is your stepmother?" She clasped Alla's hand in both of hers. "Stay."

Alla reluctantly slipped free. "And what would I do here?" She spun on the spot, her arms wide. "This is a lovely place, but my skills are limited and I'm willing to bet you've servants aplenty."

Princess Viktoriya tipped forward on the stone slab, rocking onto her feet. "Did I mention I'm looking for a wife?"

She had a vague recollection of the topic cycling through their conversation. "What does that have to do with—?" More heat flooded her face, making her dizzy even as her heart leapt. "*Me?*" She must've come to the wrong conclusion. The future ruler of the empire was *not* proposing to her. "I'm certain the empire deserves more than an orphaned half-breed as its future tsarina."

And yet, Princess Viktoriya didn't rush to reaffirm Alla was wrong. If anything, the princess seemed almost hurt. "What the empire deserves is someone who is kind and selfless." She stepped closer. "Who considers the safety of others and knows the worth in even the smallest of her people."

Alla shook her head. With as much allure as the idea had, she couldn't give up on the last vestiges of family she possessed.

"If you stay here—with me—they'll never be able to hurt you again," Princess Viktoriya insisted. "You'll be safe."

Safe. She barely remembered the feeling. Soft and cosy. Warm.

"*I* will," she whispered. "But what of those I love? Those I leave behind?" It wouldn't take much for her stepmother to deduce who was behind Alla's disappearance. "How can I linger here knowing she'll beat those whose only crimes were that they cared too much for my happiness and helped me get here tonight?"

"I am grateful to them for risking their lives. But I don't like the idea of you going back there, not after all you've told me."

"I have to." Her gaze swung to the oasis, sliding over the moon's reflection to the darker patches of the lilies breaking the image of the moon as a whole. "I think she murdered my mother." Or orchestrated it at the very least.

The princess jerked back. "What? Do you have proof?"

Alla shook her head. She had nothing beyond an unsettling feeling in the pit of her stomach. Maybe there was something still within the mansion, but she doubted it.

Princess Viktoriya softly growled a curse. "Then I can't detain her."

"Detain?"

The woman spread her arms wide. "I am the one and only heir to the Niholian throne. I can, on a whim, although it would be tricky to explain to my father."

And, no doubt, cause a scene. "What of her daughters?" They were just as much of a threat.

Frowning, the princess shook her head. "It would be even more difficult."

"Then it is best if I simply return home." Even without proof of murder, there were other things that she knew her stepmother capable of. "I don't want to think of what horrors she might inflict on Uda and Odette." And if poor Mady was discovered without Alla there to defend her?

She could barely bring herself to consider it.

"I am truly unhappy about this. Would it not be safer for me to have these people you're concerned about brought here?"

"It's more than just a few people." If serfs went missing, others would be punished until the truth was exposed. The only way to keep everyone safe was for Alla to face her stepmother. "I must go. I need to be back before they return." She couldn't risk being caught on the road, not after her earlier outburst. A lashing would be the least to worry about.

"How? By foot? If they arrived in a carriage, you'll never make it."

She wouldn't. "I have to try." Getting there to face her punishment was better than letting the others face her stepmother alone.

Sighing, Princess Viktoriya linked their fingers. She deftly guided Alla through the undergrowth around the oasis to the gardens of cultivated bushes and trees. "Then take one of my horses. You've ridden, I assume?"

"Not for a very long time." Her father had forbidden her since her mother's death. "But I couldn't possibly relieve you of—"

"If you are adamant on returning, then I'm afraid I shall have to insist."

They stepped through an archway. Alla breathed in the scent of herbs. Pungent spices that she could identify danced alongside unfamiliar ones. Fruit trees dotted the space and vines climbed the walls. The back of the palace loomed high over the garden, light glowing from nearby windows and an open door. The bustle of a busy kitchen clanged in the darkness.

Princess Viktoriya continued to guide her, leaving the kitchen garden and ushering her towards the squat bulk of the stables. The princess' footsteps crunched in the gravel whilst Alla followed silently behind, clutching her shoes.

The stable doors were big enough to admit a carriage and swung open at the slightest of tugs. Inside, the moon cast its light over the first few steps before darkness reclaimed its territory. Soft snorts and the hesitant stomp of hooves drifted from the shadows.

Alla knew the source came from the waking horses, yet still, she shuddered.

"We must be swift." Princess Viktoriya extended her arm. A globe of yellow light formed above her palm. "And quiet if we don't wish to wake the stable hands." She nodded to the loft above them, full of hay. No doubt, people slept within.

They pressed deeper into the stables. The building was easily twice as long as the one back home, stretching out into the gloom far beyond the light globe's influence. Stall doors lined either side and horse's heads appeared above them. The horses stretched their necks, lipping at the air or merely snuffling as Alla followed the princess.

"Here." The Princess hauled open one of the stall doors and slipped in with the leggy chestnut horse. "Hand me that bridle. It's on that hook there." She jerked her thumb at where a pair of bridles gleamed dully in the light.

Alla snatched the closest one and handed it over before the stall door finished swinging shut. She waited for the princess to have secured the horse before opening the stall door wide.

Princess Viktoriya led the animal out. "Now then," she whispered, peering into the gloom. "If I just knew where they kept the saddles..."

Alla had a fair idea. At least, if the stable master was the same logical type of person as the man back home. They'd be tucked safe in a room near the entrance. "There's no time." Depending on how much ground the horse could cover, or how fit it was, she already ran the risk of being caught before she reached her family's estate.

Taking the reins from the woman, Alla led the animal out of the stables. In the moonlight, the horse looked far bigger than the ponies she had learnt to ride. Could she even get on? She was no stranger to riding bareback, but the animal was very high off the ground.

"Hold on." Princess Viktoriya trotted back into the stables. She returned swiftly with a small canvas bag. "It might still have a little feed in the bottom, but—"

"Thank you." Alla took the bag and carefully lowered the shoes in before handing the bag back. There was the chance of them clanking together as she rode, but it was better than trying to hold on to them whilst trotting down the road.

The princess lingered at the horse's side, assisting Alla aboard with a boost. "I fear I shan't get another time to say this," she said whilst handing up the shoes. "But I'm pretty sure I'm falling for you."

Alla felt a smile stretching her lips before she could restrain herself. "If I may be frank, your highness?"

Princess Viktoriya ducked her head, although no amount of shadows could hide her grin. "Have you been anything else since we met?

"You barely know me."

"And what are my chances of getting to know more about you than I have on this night? You kiss like one possessed, yet are all set to vanish like the morning mist. Will I ever see you again? Or shall I need to personally track you down and chase out your demons?"

Morning. When her stepmother would return to the estate. Yes, a single horse would be faster than the camels dragging the carriage, but she needed time to don her ruined gown and clamber the mansion into the attic. She had to leave now if she was to be back where the woman expected her.

Alla nudged the horse forward a few steps before whirling the animal around. "Meet me in the market square tomorrow at sundown? Near the fountain where we first met." She wasn't sure how she was going to explain the horse's appearance back home, but she could at least return the beast to its owner.

"I shall breathlessly await your arrival." The princess clasped Alla's fingers, squeezing them briefly before stepping back. "Now go. Quickly. And be safe."

Kicking the horse into a gallop, Alla tore across the palace grounds, aiming for the gate. Odette and Uda would be long since gone, but if the horse was able to maintain a steady trot once they left the city, she might just catch up with them.

Chapter 12

The clouds were just beginning to grow light as the familiar shape of the estate gates came into view. *Almost there.* Alla clung tightly to the reins, summoning every scrap of long-abandoned horsemanship to stay on the animal's back.

The cart also hadn't been at the rendezvous point. She had hoped to not be too far behind Odette and Uda, but the roads had remained clear the entire way home. It could mean they hadn't lingered rather than something nefarious. She hoped so. Surely the palace guards were being extra vigilant tonight, especially with the entirety of the empire's nobility in attendance. They wouldn't allow any criminal act to happen within shouting distance of the walls.

Her shoulders sagged as the horse shuffled through the gates, the steady clip-clop of hooves pounding through her head. *Home.* Just the climb up the mansion awaited her. Her backside ached as did her legs. She had travelled such a distance on her own two feet, but never atop an animal. How she longed for sleep beneath the blissful cocoon of blankets.

Such rest wouldn't be hers to claim. Her stepmother would believe she had spent the night in the attic, not gallivanting around the palace grounds with Princess Viktoriya.

She smiled at the thought of the princess. *Vik.* So sweet and gentle. So eager to see Alla again. The kiss they had shared loomed in her mind, the memory of those soft lips, the brush of the princess' thumb on her ear… it tingled along her skin and warmed her to the core.

Had Princess Viktoriya been serious about searching for a wife? *Of course.* Everyone knew the future ruler had yet to choose a bride. But for it to be *Alla?*

She shook her head. She could spend days running her thoughts in circles without coming to an answer. *I'll know tomorrow.* Even if the possibility of marriage was merely the festivities and moonlight talking, the princess' offer for Alla to stay in the palace showed promise. Perhaps she could find employment in the kitchen or the garden.

But that kiss...

Sighing as the scene continued on in her mind's eye, she rounded the mansion to find the stable doors open and the cart nestled in the back. At least she could be sure Odette and Uda made it home. One small worry removed.

The stable master was tending to some of the tack, the stable hands having already left to harness the camels for their daily work in the fields. He eyed Alla as she halted before the doors. "Since when did we have a horse?" He tipped his head, giving the animal a critical onceover. "I'd say he's quite well-bred, too. Did you find him out on the road, Miss?"

"Something like that," she mumbled, dismounting and leading the horse inside. She should've considered a plausible story for the animal's sudden appearance, but her mind was slush. "I'm taking him back in the afternoon." Providing she had enough strength left after a day of her usual work.

Or maybe her stepmother planned to leave her locked away in the attic as punishment. It would certainly give her the time she needed to rest. *And pack.* Whilst she wouldn't be able to carry much, there were a few small items from her parents that she had tucked away.

But first...

Her gaze slid to the attic window. Just thinking of the climb made her tired. *Change first.* She'd never make it up there in her current attire anyway. And being caught in her stepsister's clothes? Unthinkable. But, with the other two back, maybe she had time to change before—

The jingle of a harness caught her ear.

Alla spun, certain her heart had leapt into her throat, only to realise the sound had come from within the stables. *Calm.* It was just the stable master turning the harness over on the rack. The carriage hadn't returned. But it could. And soon.

She pressed the horse's reins into the stable master's grasp. "Would you be able to look after him until later?"

He nodded and gently shooed her out of the stables with a flap of his free hand. "I'll see that he's cared for, Miss. Off you trot. This is no place for a gown like that."

Alla ran for the kitchen door, clutching the feed bag before her to keep the shoes from clinking. The ground between the stables and the mansion was soiled in places by the leavings of ducks and chickens, tracking any of into the building would definitely leave a suspicious trail. Skirting every spot whilst maintaining a swift pace wasn't her usual skill, but she somehow managed to reach the door and fling it open with one hand.

Odette dove to one side, holding a pot high above her head. "My lady?" She lowered the intended weapon almost as swiftly and took the feed bag from Alla's arms. "We thought the worst."

A harrumph issued from the corner as Uda lurched to her feet, carrying a small bundle that looked to be Alla's clothes. Beyond the three of them, the kitchen was strangely empty. Had they seen her arrival and ushered everyone out? She didn't think any of the serfs would willingly offer up information.

"You're cutting it fine," Uda muttered, helping Alla remove the overdress.

"I lost track of the time." She'd still some of it left. Maybe enough to attempt the climb up the mansion.

Uda gave another grumbling snort. "You'll lose track of a lot more if we can't get you back where the Mistress expects you to be." The overdress was tossed to one side as if the fine threads were rags. The underdress came off with less fuss, enabling Alla to slip into the first layer of her own clothes.

Mady erupted through the door, panting and signing wildly. "They're back!"

Alla doubled her efforts to dress. Even if she forsook the outer layer and started her climb to the attic, she would still be caught. Her stepmother would certainly check there first. Spotting Alla's absence, and the open window, would be as simple as opening the hatch.

Uda rushed around the kitchen, grabbed the discarded gown and hastened out the door, no doubt to conceal the garments in some pile of dirty laundry Alla's stepsisters always managed to accumulate in their room. It didn't matter how short a time the pair had worn a garment, once it had touched their bodies, they deemed it for the laundry.

"I don't know how we're going to spin you being out and about when the mistress clearly locked you away," Odette said.

"*We* aren't," Alla hissed as she fussed with the final tie. "You need to leave. Both of you," she added upon spying Mady still lurking nearby. "Go wait with the others. I'll handle my stepmother."

Odette took a few steps towards the door, the gentle clink of glass drawing Alla's attention to the feed bag.

The shoes. She couldn't risk letting the women hold onto the shoes. Claiming the feed bag from Odette, she searched for a place to stash it until she could return the items to their original places. *Somewhere discreet.* But where could she expect her stepsisters not to go?

"Mady dear, wait." Alla motioned the girl closer, bundling the glass shoes into the girl's arms, feed bag and all. "Take these. Carefully. That's it. Hide them in the cellar. And yourself. Quickly."

The girl scuttled off, pausing in the doorway only long enough to glance back at Alla.

She gave Mady her best, brightest and bravest smile. Whatever punishment her stepmother doled out, it was going to hurt. But that didn't mean Mady should be frightened. Those who worked within the mansion kitchen would see to the girl's safety.

A faint twinge of guilt hit her gut at the thought. If she left for the palace, there would be no one standing between them and her stepmother. She had never been able to do more than take the brunt of the woman's anger, but it was something.

Could she take Mady with her? The horse could carry both of them readily enough, especially if she kept an easy pace. Would it be fair to take the girl from where she seemed to be settling in so well? There was still the danger of her being caught, though. That could increase once Alla left. *She'll have to come.* There was no other option to keep her out of danger.

Hopefully, the princess wouldn't mind.

Alla had originally returned to stop her stepmother from using people like Odette and Uda as a means to quell her temper. She wasn't about to idly stand by whilst another remained in danger.

" 'Dett?" she said upon realising the woman still shared the room. "You need to leave."

Odette opened her mouth and, for a moment, Alla thought the woman would object to leaving her to face her punishment alone. Then she bowed her head and left the kitchen, wedging the external door open on her way out.

Tying the final bit of her bodice lace, Alla took in the room. She'd never seen it devoid of all people beyond herself. Strange how hollow it seemed without the usual bustle and chatter, like the heart had been ripped out of the mansion.

Alla fussed with setting the kettle over a freshly lit fire in preparation of a soothing peppermint tea, then prepared a tray with a few delicacies left over from last night's dinner. All the while, she kept one ear trained on the scuffling activity beyond the door leading out into the mansion's main corridors.

How much warning would she get? It seemed too still for the arrival Mady claimed. Perhaps the girl was wrong and the carriage was a visitor who would expect some form of nourishment this early in the day.

But the longer things remained quiet, the more her stomach churned. She glanced at each entryway into the kitchen. Nothing but whispers of movement drifted through the main entrance. The doorway leading upstairs remained closed, but it was unlikely her stepmother would enter that way. The external door?

The open doorway beckoned her.

Alla inched towards the exit. She could be up the first story in a heartbeat, perhaps climb all the way to the top before either her stepmother or stepsisters were aware. Especially if they were inside.

"I don't care if it takes several hours to cook the blasted things," Natalya screeched, her voice growing louder. "It shouldn't matter if I'm not in bed. They should know I'm hungry and have it ready for me."

Closing her eyes, Alla breathed deep in an attempt to still

the fluttering in her stomach. She knew what her stepsister was after, the usual wakeup snack of puffed pastry and whipped cream. That wasn't an issue. The tray she had prepared would suffice, but the fact Natalya's voice was getting nearer was troubling.

The door opened. Her stepmother halted in the entrance, not even moving when both of her daughters crowded into the doorway.

"Mistress," Alla said, acknowledging their presence with a curtsy. She glided nonchalantly to the fireplace. She was merely waiting for the kettle to pipe its usual song of readiness. *There's nothing else to be concerned about.* If she believed it, then maybe they would, too. "Stepsisters."

Natalya pressed into the room, her gaze solely for the tray of food on the counter. She was halted by her mother's clawed grip on her shoulder.

Alla's stepmother eyed her like a vulture spying a sand viper. "My dear daughters," she cooed, caressing Tamara's cheek. "Do leave us."

"But Mother," Natalya bleated. She raised a hand, almost imploring the food to come to her. A single pastry did wobble its way off the table to float into the air.

It fell as Alla's stepmother batted away Natalya's hand. "Now."

Alla watched her stepsisters flinch and scramble, obeying the curt command. Not once had she seen her stepmother raise a hand to her own children, but she did wonder from time to time. "Is something wrong?"

"Wrong?" her stepmother snarled. "*Wrong?*" She stalked across the kitchen floor, her gaze intent on Alla. "Of course nothing is *wrong.* Just some grubby little elven tart dancing with the princess as though she'd the right to be there."

Alla stepped back. Her skin prickled, her flesh crawling over her bones. "There was an elf at the ball?"

The external entry was to her left. A quick dash if she could round the table. The horse would still be in the stables.

She shuffled a slow step in that direction. "How unusual to see—"

The door slammed shut with enough force to crack its thick glass window. "It was *you,* wasn't it?" her stepmother hissed. "I don't need to ask how you managed to escape the attic. I will deal with *those* insubordinates later."

Alla straightened. She had hoped, after having a pleasant evening out, her stepmother would've forgotten having locked her away. *Clearly not.* But she wasn't about to let anyone else suffer alongside her. "If you look, you will find the hatch is locked and a window is wide open. No one helped me."

She peered at Alla from beneath her lashes, her nose held high. "It *was* you at the ball, then. I wasn't certain until I saw you here." She glanced around the kitchen, no doubt looking for a sign of others and the hastily shed clothes. "You must have had help."

"No help," Alla repeated. "Just my own ingenuity." She needed her stepmother to believe her.

Her stepmother scoffed. "*You?*" She strode closer, her steps like that of a cat stalking a field mouse. "You've no smarts, girl. Do you think you could hide it from me? That I wouldn't be able to pick out my daughter's dress draped over your scrawny frame?" She grabbed Alla's arm, the grip all but crushing her wrist. "And, of all the ridiculous things, to dance with the empire's *heir*? Do you realise how that would've looked? What they would've done if they had found out one of my—"

"One of your... *what?*" she snarled, knowing full well what words were going to come out of her stepmother's mouth. "I'm not one of your anything, am I? My father would be horrified at what you've done. *I* have barely stomached it." But only because she had thought herself helpless. "Then again, what do I know? I'm just a half-breed, yes? Lesser than both?" She shook her head, blinking back tears. "No matter what you think, my mother was not less than you. No. I tell a lie. She was *better*. And I had every right to be there." Even if she hadn't personally been given the invitation, she was of noble blood, no different than her stepsisters.

"You should've been thrown into the palace dungeon." Her grip on Alla's arm tightened further. Heat from the woman's palm seared her skin.

Alla whimpered. She tried to contain the noise, but it wormed out her throat. Tears poured down her cheeks no matter how she tried to staunch them. She stumbled as her stepmother hauled her across the room. Where was she being taken now?

"I tried, you know," her stepmother continued. "I tried to be patient, to keep you around, despite my misgivings. I didn't have to. I did it to honour your father's memory."

"Honour my father?" Alla jerked out of the woman's grasp, scuttling back. She'd no chance of outrunning the woman's magic, but her feet refused to just stand there. "You know, I used to wonder why you kept me here." If she was quick, she might make it to the door. "All the threats to sell me? They're hollow."

Her stepmother paused, her eyes narrowing.

"My father didn't leave this place to you. It's *mine*." She had mulled over it long and hard during the ride back. The deeds had to be somewhere within the mansion. One of the serfs must know. Perhaps Gerde as the woman was always poking about the upper levels. "You can't be rid of me without risking losing *my* home."

The air around her changed. Invisible bands clamped onto her legs and secured her arms. Her feet left the ground. The bands wound around her chest, stealing her breath. How much magic did it take to crush a person? The thought bounced around her head, squeezing the rest of the breath from her lungs.

"I can't?" her stepmother hissed. She stood by the door to the cellar, toying with the key jutting from the lock. "I think you'll find that I can." She flung the door open into darkness.

Alla swiftly found herself launched into the black maw.

She hit the ground and lay still, struggling to breathe, the air knocked from her lungs. Her whole body screamed. The taste and smell of blood invaded her senses—a cut lip. Other stings and pangs worked their way across her skin.

"I tried doing it the nice way," her stepmother said from the doorway. "But now you've gone and done it. You've officially become more trouble than you're worth. Enjoy your stay. It'll be your last memory of this place." She slammed the door, sealing away all but a few dregs of light.

When she could breathe again, Alla limped her way back up the stairs. She pounded on the door, the thump of solid wood echoing through the room. Pulling down on the latch garnered only the faint clunk of locked metal. It was about what she had expected.

She slumped against the door, sliding down the wood to huddle upon the steps.

This was it. Locked in the darkness with only the rats for company. Did her stepmother expect her to starve? Or did she have something else in mind?

Chapter 13

Alla sat with her back pressed into the corner of the cellar nearest the lift. It was also the farthest she could get from the door without attempting to tunnel her way through the brick lining the room. Had she the ability, she would've tried.

She had discovered Mady still in the room a few hours after being locked in here, cowering in this same spot. Sending the girl up via the lift had taken some time with her hauling every inch, terrified the old ropes would snap under the lean weight of a child.

Two days. That was how long she had been down here alone, the time measured by the sound drifting down the lift from the kitchen. Opening the door without the key was impossible. She'd given it numerous attempts, from breaking the old planks to assaulting the rusty hinges. Those on the other side had attempted the same. Yedivy had even tried picking the lock to no avail.

There had to be some way they hadn't thought of. It was the only way out. She couldn't cram herself into the lift as she had done with Mady. No matter how Alla tried to squeeze into the little box, her legs were just too long and at least one of her elbows would stick out into the cellar. If she had still been the same small girl of seven, but those years had passed thrice over. More importantly, she had gained a foot in height since then.

At least food could be sneaked to her. What arrived on the

lift were the dregs of another's meal, nothing less than what she had lived on for years. It would pose a problem if her stepmother expected Alla to waste away, but she wasn't ready to just give up.

They had also sent down a candle stub and flint. She had briefly lit it on the first day to see her surroundings in full. The dusty floor with its empty barrels and forgotten bottles held little in the way of other comforts. At least she had the feed bag to pillow her head whilst she slept.

Her stomach grumbled a questioning note towards a forthcoming lunch. She tightened her hold on herself in an attempt to quell the noise. *Soon.* The midday meal wasn't always requested at a set time, but it would come.

The grate of a key in a lock caught her attention. Alla lifted her head as the door creaked open. A figure stood in the doorway. She couldn't make out who. Had her stepmother come for her or had one of the serfs found the key?

Squinting against the brightness, Alla slowly uncurled her limbs.

"Get up," her stepmother's order lashed through the air.

She wearily responded. Whilst she had the strength, her limbs had grown stiff with the cold and the damp.

"Quickly. Do you not wish to be free of this dismal place?" Her stepmother huffed, one hand thumping her hip, as Alla continued the sluggish pace. "Faster, girl. The market isn't open all evening."

Market? Alla halted. There was only one market her stepmother would be interested in sending her to. If she was to be sold, she would not head to such a fate willingly, regardless of whether it would see her out of the cellar.

"For the love of—" Her stepmother's irritation echoed through the cellar as she stomped down the stairs, a globe of light illuminating her path. The sickly glow glinted off something in her hand. The buckle of a collar.

Alla shuffled a half-step backwards before realising she was in a corner. The stairs were a straight run. If only her stepmother wasn't standing between her and them.

Steeling herself, she bolted for the door.

She had barely taken more than a few steps before she was thrown to the floor. Sucking down air, Alla continued on at a crawl. Something had her by the leg. It didn't matter. Stopping meant defeat.

"Don't be a fool," her stepmother snarled, hauling Alla upright on her knees. "We both know I should've done this a long time ago."

Alla thrashed her head. It did little. Magical binds twisted their way around her, pinning her arms at her side. The jingle of metal clanged in her ears. Cold leather wrapped around her throat, growing tighter for one frantic heartbeat before loosening as the buckle was done.

"Honestly," her stepmother continued, taking hold of the short leash. "The only reason I don't flay you where you stand is because the barons pay pittance for damaged goods."

Alla's hand flew to her neck in search of the buckle. She had weathered the magic-suppressing chain because she had been given no other choice and could manage without her abilities, but this? "You can't sell me. This is my estate. Sell me and you lose it."

Her stepmother laughed. "Stupid girl, you think I wouldn't think of that?" She crushed Alla's cheeks in her grip. "Such a plain face. So easy to replace. What documents are there but the deed? Your name? Easily given to some pliant girl." She marched up the stairs, dragging Alla close behind by the leash. "I'm not selling some foolish little half-breed named Alla, I'm getting rid of an unruly brat of a slave."

Alla swallowed. The leather allowed just that much. She gripped the collar, seeking to ebb the bite on her skin. All it got her were pinched fingers.

Her stepmother led her through the kitchen and down the corridors to the foyer.

Alla tugged and fought each step. She dug her heels in, even as her bare feet found no purchase. She grabbed anything that might slow the woman—doorways, furniture, even the stunned figure of a passing serf.

Her efforts yielded little more than the odd grunt or huff from her stepmother.

The door leading to outside loomed in her mind. Once she was beyond the mansion's confines, she'd have even less chance of stopping anyone from hoisting her onto the cart like a sack of flour. And once in the city? No one would even think to help her. Her only chance was to find a way to free herself from her stepmother's grasp on the leash and run.

Her stepmother opened the door.

A handful of mounted people waited in the courtyard. Every single one of them wore the blue of the royal guard. Could it be that—?

Alla took a step through the doorway but her stepmother shoved her inside. Thrown off-balance, she tumbled onto her backside.

"Your highness," her stepmother gasped. The faint rustle of fabric suggested the woman had the sense to curtsy. "How unexpected."

Princess Viktoriya was here? She couldn't recall telling the princess where she lived. Was she looking for Alla after her wait in the marketplace had been in vain? Or perhaps the horse she hadn't returned. "Vik!" she screamed, scrambling for the entrance.

The door slammed shut, her stepmother on the opposite side.

"It is such an honour for you to appear at my humble abode," her stepmother continued in an overloud tone. "To what do I owe your visit?"

"I am actually on a hunt," Princess Viktoriya replied. "A young woman I am seeking to make my wife. Goes by the name of Alla. Have you heard of her?"

"Yes!" Alla lurched towards the door. "It's me." The latch refused to budge. "I—" Her fist thumped the wood once and was stilled despite her attempts to raise it again. She went to open her mouth, to scream her loudest, except...

Her jaw refused to move.

"No, you don't," Tamara hissed in her ear. Her hand replaced the paralyses on Alla's jaw. She dragged Alla away from the door. "I think it's back into the cellar for you."

"I'm afraid," her stepmother said. She must've heard Alla's response. Had the princess? "There is no one living here by that name."

I'm right here. Any words Alla dared to utter became only muffled noise too quiet for human ears to pick up. She thrashed against Tamara's grip. For all her stepsister's preferences to lounge about, she was surprisingly strong.

"Can I interest you in staying for tea?" her stepmother offered. "My two daughters should be done with their lessons."

If Princess Viktoriya gave an answer, Alla was too far away to hear it.

She struggled, reaching for the door handle. If she could gain another step, another inch of leeway, the door would be hers. But Tamara clung tight, hauling her further away.

Still, she tried. Freedom was so close. She had to let Princess Viktoriya know.

I'm here.

Chapter 14

Tamara dragged her down the same corridor Alla's stepmother had towed her. All activity within the kitchen stopped when they entered.

Alla glanced around, noting a small figure darting behind the skirts of the twins. Mady was safe, then. What of Odette and Uda? The pair weren't usually in the kitchen at this hour, so not seeing them meant nothing as to their fates. Perhaps her stepmother believed she had acted alone.

"Get back to work," Tamara snapped, opening the cellar. "As for you." She whipped Alla back like an empty sack and flung her towards the doorway. "Down you go."

Alla pitched into the darkness. She tumbled down the stairs with a shriek, hitting every single step and sprawling upon the floor. The door was already shut. Faint light peeked around the edges, but not enough to see by.

She stared into the blackness high above, slowly regaining her breath and waiting for the pain to adjust to something bearable. Her left hip ached. Not broken, but certainly more battered than the right. Fresh scratches and scrapes adorned her arms and legs. They stung with the smallest of movements.

"This really isn't necessary," her stepmother's voice echoed from somewhere to her left.

Alla rocked her head, frowning at the lift. Were they in the kitchen? Had Princess Viktoriya insisted on a tour? Her stepmother certainly wouldn't be showing the princess around out of goodwill. She rarely ventured beyond a few rooms within the mansion on a regular day.

"It is," Princess Viktoriya replied.

Hauling herself to her feet, Alla limped up the stairs. Her body objected to the task, huffing and grunting at every step. At the top, she pounded on the door. "I'm in here!"

The silence that followed settled like lead in her stomach.

"Sorry, my lady," Yedivy answered. "They've gone to the dining room."

Alla leant against the door.

She's looking for me. That had to be the only reason Princess Viktoriya hadn't left. Alerting her to Alla's presence within the mansion should be enough. But how? What could she possibly do from down here? Since Alla hadn't returned with—

The horse.

Was it still in the stables? She couldn't imagine her stepmother doing away with an obviously well-bred animal. Selling, perhaps. But that would take time. "Go to the stables," she yelled through the door, hoping Yedivy heard her as clearly as she did he. "Tell the stable master that Mistress Antonina has requested it be led out into the courtyard." There should be a few of the riders still outside. Hopefully, one of them would recognise the horse.

"At once, my lady," Yedivy answered.

Alla settled on the top step. If that option didn't work, then what else? Wait and hope? She'd been doing that for far too long. What else was she capable of doing?

The lift rattled, ascending to deliver tea and snacks up to the dining room.

Scuttling down the stairs, Alla hauled open the lift hatch. With the lift itself far above, the chute was little more than a giant echoing chamber. "Vik!"

Her ears strained to hear any sort of reply. Nothing.

She can't hear me. Why would she? There must be all sorts of noise coming from the kitchen that would drown out Alla's voice. If they had even reached the dining room, yet.

Alla flopped against the wall. There had to be something she could do, something she could send. *Something of mine.* But what? All she had down here was herself and she had already tried—

The shoes.

She scrabbled in the darkness. She had removed them from the feed bag on the first night. Her stepmother hadn't mentioned them when she dragged Alla up the stairs, which meant they were probably still tucked in the corner where she had slept.

Her groping fingers alighted on one cool heel, then another. Would it be enough? She had mentioned to the princess that they were borrowed. Would Princess Viktoriya remember?

Hand over hand, she coaxed the lift down. The rope slid and jerked in her hands, further abrading her already scraped palms. Voices echoed down the chute, too jumbled for her to make any sense of. She hoped it meant Princess Viktoriya had chosen to humour Alla's stepmother.

The murmurs continued even as she set both shoes on the lift and hoisted it back up.

The lift wouldn't go all the way, not from the cellar. Someone in the kitchen would have to pull the latch or personally carry the shoes up. *Mady*. The princess remembered Alla rescuing the girl, perhaps she would also recognise her. And if Mady was to arrive holding a shoe?

She scrambled for the door, calling out for the girl as she climbed.

An answering rap on the wood greeted her.

"Mady, I need you to do something for me." It would be risky. If her stepmother or stepsisters intervened before Princess Viktoriya spotted the girl... *No*. It was too dangerous of an ask. "Remember the shoes I had you hide? They're in the lift. When I tug on the rope, you hit the latch and let it go up. All right?"

Another, shorter, knock followed.

Alla limped down the stairs, almost tumbling part of the way. She grasped the rope and tugged.

The dull thud of the latch answered her and the lift moved. The voices high above continued. At least they seemed to have settled in the dining room.

Finally, the rope refused to travel up any further. Alla sat back, keeping a steadying hand on the rope lest one of the kitchen staff tried to summon the lift. All she could do now was wait and hope someone checked the lift.

"There's that noise again," exclaimed a deep voice, clear and loud.

"As I said earlier," her stepmother replied. "It's just the lift. I'm sure it's merely one of the servants sending down the dishes or some forgotten—"

"Your highness," that same deep voice announced. It didn't sound familiar. One of the royal guards? "There appears to be a shoe in here."

"That's mine," Natalya shrieked. "What's it doing—?"

Alla screamed the princess' name, trying for every high-pitched note she could reach and straining for those her throat simply couldn't make. Only when the certainty of unconsciousness loomed did she stop to take another breath.

"What in the world?" the deep voice rumbled down the chute. "I think there's someone down there."

A muffled objection bounced its way to her ears. Her stepmother? One of her stepsisters? Perhaps all three? It was hard to tell through the echoes.

"What is that child doing in here?" her stepmother demanded, her sharp voice cutting through the jabber.

"And with *my* shoe?" Natalya added.

Another voice silenced the protests, the tone familiar even though the words weren't clear. Princess Viktoriya.

Alla steadied her breathing in preparation for another scream. If anything, it would drive them outside to where the horse would be waiting. When the echoes of that wail died, she let forth with another. And another.

The pause between each to regain her breath grew longer. If they didn't come soon, she might pass out. Something she couldn't risk. Who knew where she would wake up?

Last one. She swallowed, willing away the pain in her throat. Would she even be able to speak after this?

A crunching, grating noise reverberated through the cellar. Alla cocked her head and listened. That was definitely—

The key to the lock turned with a dreadful clunk. The door swung open. A bright globe of light flooded the cellar, shining on the cobwebs and sending the rats scurrying for the shadows.

"As her highness can see," her stepmother said. "There's nothing and no one of import here. Shall we head back up?"

Alla barely heard the woman.

Princess Viktoriya stood in the doorway garbed in the same

handsome blue shirt and trousers she'd worn the day they had met in the market square. She glowed with the energy of a goddess. "Alla?"

Alla staggered for the steps. Her princess—her Vik—had come for her. She was here. *Actually* here. Tears poured down her face, turning the world into a shimmering mess of little orbs of light.

Viktoriya met her halfway up the stairs. "Alla," she whispered. "My beautiful, strong Alla." She delicately pressed her lips to Alla's cheek. "I said I would find you again."

Unable to stop crying, Alla clung to the princess, burying her face into the woman's chest.

"Her highness must be confused," her stepmother insisted, still lingering in the doorway. "This is..." She cocked her head, a smirk gracing her lips for a moment. "Little Soot. Naught but an unruly thief and liar who is due to be sent off to where she'll be of some use."

"No," Princess Viktoriya murmured. "I know that face. Bruised though it is." She cupped Alla's cheeks. The tingle of magic flowed through her fingers, wrapping Alla in soothing warmth even as the princess drew Alla into her arms.

Alla tightened her hold, the aches across her body subsiding, washed away by the princess' healing magic.

"But, your highness," her stepmother exclaimed. "The shoe..." She gestured at Mady who stood calmly at the woman's side. The girl's chest puffed out in pride as she clutched one of the glass shoes. "You said the woman you were looking for wore them, but they couldn't possibly fit her. And my daughter—"

Princess Viktoriya laughed. "Those shoes never did fit." She smiled warmly at Alla. "But I don't need them to tell me what my heart already knows. Whether garbed in the finest of silks or dressed in rags, I would know her wherever. How could I ever forget my gentle and kind Alla?" She stepped back, drawing them into the natural light beaming through the kitchen windows.

A sigh slipped from Alla's lips. That pale golden glow was the most lustrous sight. She knelt before Mady and drew the girl close. "Thank you," she whispered.

Keeping a hand on Mady's shoulder, Alla followed at Princess Viktoriya's side as they left the kitchen for the foyer.

A pair of guards marched at their backs, undoubtedly Ghosts.

And, trotting behind them like bewildered puppies, came her stepmother and stepsisters.

"She was *looking* for Alla?" Tamara asked. "Are we sure she's actually the princess?"

"And what was Soot doing with *my* shoes?" Natalya demanded.

"Stealing them, obviously," Alla's stepmother hissed, her voice low. "You saw how she clung to the woman. How she couldn't wait to get her greedy lips on that mouth. She's just as much a conniving little tart as her mother."

Princess Viktoriya halted, whirling on the woman. "Is it common for you to speak ill of the dead?"

"*Elven* dead," Alla's stepmother stressed. She jerked her chin in Alla's direction. "I hope you're aware of her breeding. Creatures like her are barely worth a grave, never mind a crown. If it's a lady her highness is looking to wed, both of my two wonderful daughters are well-bred and available. Why, my eldest can—" She fell silent as Princess Viktoriya held up her hand.

"I've heard enough about you and your daughters."

"You have?" Her dark gaze darted Alla's way. "All good things I trust?"

Alla scrunched her shoulders, trying to make herself smaller still, before realising she needn't have bothered. Uncertainty dominated her stepmother's face, along with a touch of fear.

"They were *enlightening* things," Princess Viktoriya curtly answered, turning her back on the woman. "Lady Alla, I came here with the intention of making you my bride, but it occurs to me that I never actually asked." She held out her hand. "So, would you do me the honour?"

"Don't you dare answer," her stepmother hissed. "I forbid it."

"Yes." The word was out before Alla could think. She had spoken truly when she pointed out how little they knew of each other, but if the princess saw no qualms in wedding a half-breed—even going as far as tracking Alla down—then why not? She clasped the proffered hand. "I will."

"*This* is what the world has come to?" her stepmother grumbled, folding her arms firmly across her chest. "I hope you don't expect any sort of dowry to go with that tramp."

Not turning her gaze from Alla, Princess Viktoriya smirked. "And what could my Alla possibly want that I cannot give her?"

"Odette and Uda," Alla replied. She couldn't walk away from her family home whilst knowing they were still under her stepmother's care. There was little she could do about those the woman had bought, but freeing those two would be a start.

Her stepmother frowned. "Who?"

Princess Viktoriya raised a brow. "They would be the serfs you left my side for?"

Alla nodded. She didn't know what had become of them. Nothing bad, she hoped. "Please," she implored of the princess. "They belonged to my father's household. I would prefer to have them with me as my personal servants. And Mady." She gave the girl's shoulder a reassuring squeeze.

"If that is your wish. It *is* your estate and they are under your care." Princess Viktoriya turned to the royal guards shadowing the princess' every movement. "Find these women Lady Alla mentioned and have them brought to the courtyard."

"*Her* estate?" Alla's stepmother shrieked. "Is that what she told you? It's not *hers*. Who would leave such a rich resource to a half-breed?"

Princess Viktoriya's jaw twitched. "Inform them," she continued to her guards as if she hadn't been interrupted, "that they are to be removed from all ownership and are free to remain under Lady Alla's employ. And see that this screeching woman is contained."

The guard thumped her chest. "Your will shall be done, your highness." She grabbed Alla's stepmother, hooking her hand into the crook of the woman's arm. "Come, my lady."

"You can't do that," Alla's stepmother said, pulling away from the guard to face Princess Viktoriya. She planted herself firmly before the princess, glowering with all her might. "They belong to *me*. This is *my* estate."

Alla held her breath and huddled behind the other guard. Such an expression from her stepmother was so often followed by a lashing that Alla's back tensed at the very sight.

The princess countered the stare with a cool look. "I'm certain you're unused to hearing such, but you are wrong. Alla owns the deed and any other property that was originally her father's, which I hear you have abused in your regency." She glanced at Alla. "Alongside other atrocities."

"Are you telling me a half-breed gets the right over a wife?"

"A daughter over a *second* wife," Princess Viktoriya amended.

"And what of *my* daughters? Of myself?" She stalked towards Alla, but the guard blocked her path. "After the shelter I've given you, you would see us destitute? Have us living on the streets?"

"You would see me sold to a glass baron," Alla gently reminded the woman. The collar and leash still hung around her neck. "Speaking of which..." She carefully unbuckled the leather strap and dumped it at her stepmother's feet. "I believe this is yours."

"And let us not forget," Princess Viktoriya added. "How you outright lied to your future tsarina and attempted to obstruct my search. Both grave offences."

Her stepmother shrunk from the princess' stare. Had it finally dawned on her the trouble her vitriol caused? "I—"

"I think it's clear what needs to be done." Princess Viktoriya turned to the other guard. "Ivan, have Countess Antonina and her daughters escorted to the palace."

Her stepmother straightened, a self-satisfied little smile upon her lips.

"And ensure the countess is sent to fight on the northern border as soon as the tides allow," commanded Princess Viktoriya. "Oh, and ensure she is contained immediately upon her arrival to the palace."

"The northern—" Terror widened her stepmother's eyes, her mouth dropping open in stunned disbelief. "You... you can't."

Princess Viktoriya rounded on the woman. The cool smugness in her smile sent a thrill of heat trembling through Alla's body.

"I mean," her stepmother gabbled. "Her highness is well within her rights to order whatever she wishes. I merely ask that you consider mercy, if not for myself, then for my daughters. Surely, you do not seek to send them with me? The northern border would be a death sentence for such gentle women."

"And selling Alla would've been the same for her, yet you clearly didn't mind there. Alla?" Princess Viktoriya turned to her. "You are the slighted party in all this. Do they deserve my mercy?"

Her stepmother's gaze alighted on her, stripped of their coldness for perhaps the first time since Alla had met the woman.

"Mercy?" Alla echoed.

"Mother!" Natalya wailed. She darted through the group, clasping Alla's shoulders in a tight hug. "How could you sell Alla?"

"You know how dear our stepsister is to us," Tamara added, hastening to join in.

"Ladies, control yourselves," Princess Viktoriya snapped. She waved a hand and the guards dragged the sisters away.

Alla's gaze slid to her stepmother. "What was it you used to say?" she mused aloud. "That mercy must be earned?"

Her stepsisters stilled, terror widening their eyes.

"I think," Alla continued, "they should be shown all the kindness and mercy they afforded to me."

Her stepmother sank to her knees.

Princess Viktoriya nodded. "As you decree. Send them, too."

"But we've done nothing," Tamara said.

Alla opened her mouth, an objection to their lies on her tongue.

"Wickedness," said Princess Viktoriya, "comes not only from those who wield the whip, but also in those who hold the power to stop injustice and choose not to. Either one of you had the chance. Your lack of compassion stains your souls to the core." She offered her arm to Alla. "Come, my dear, I think we've tarried here long enough. Let us gather your family and be off."

Family? She hadn't ever considered it in such terms, but she supposed it was true. Neither Odette nor Uda could've looked after her any better than if she had been their child. But family didn't own each other. Setting them free of their tie to the estate, and her ownership, was long overdue.

Alla glanced at her stepmother, no longer more than a weeping woman. "She's never coming back, is she?"

"Never," Princess Viktoriya said. "You are safe. No one will ever harm you again. On this, I swear."

"Then yes." She laid a hand in the crook of the princess' arm. "Let's go home."

Chapter 15

Alla nervously linked and unlinked her fingers, trying not to squirm as Ivan, the human Ghost standing before her, examined the magic-negating chain around her neck. He hummed and clicked his tongue as his fingers worked along each link, searching for the seam that would part under his touch. Her gaze flicked from the bland cream-coloured ceiling to his face.

His expression told her nothing. It hardly ever did.

She'd been adamant on the chain's removal since learning the metal was unstable and could explode at the smallest upset. Even the revelation that said removal would prove euphoric and leave her emotions raw did nothing to dissuade her. She was safe, in the company of those she trusted.

Alla hadn't imagined it would take this long. Her back was starting to hurt from standing so still and straight.

She stood in the middle of her chambers in the palace. Hers. Actually *hers*. Ostensibly, she was the princess' guest, but everyone seemed to know about her and the upcoming wedding.

It was a few months away, but her insides still bubbled— happy, giddy bubbles that made her giggle at the slightest thought of it. Never would she have considered marriage, certainly not to royalty. But here she was, their upcoming union blessed by the tsar himself. She was to become the wife of Princess Viktoriya.

You're doing it again, she gently chided. Viktoriya was

adamant Alla try to think of her with no title. She was simply Vik.

"Found it," Ivan announced. He glanced over her shoulder where her betrothed lingered, then met Alla's gaze. "Ready, my lady?"

Was she? Viktoriya seemed insistent that those whose magic was contained sensed the world in muted shades. Alla couldn't recall any difference from the memories of her childhood. Nothing from back then had seemed particularly bright.

She wished Odette or Uda were here. But of the two women she had freed from lifelong serfdom, only the elven one of the pair had opted to remain by her side. Uda had gone in search of her son, a child Alla hadn't been aware of. Alla had kept track of Uda's movements, and tried to help where she could, but it seemed the woman hadn't much luck in tracking him down.

Whereas Odette was currently a translator for Mady's endless questions as the girl bounced around the palace grounds, off after whatever gripped her interest that day. Last week, it had been the stables. Today, it was the gardens, the oasis specifically.

Steeling herself, Alla gave the Ghost a curt nod. "I'm ready."

Ivan's hands twitched. There was a faint snap, like the breaking of a thin twig, and the chain slithered off her neck. A faint pressure in her mind disappeared just as smoothly.

Alla blinked. The muted cream of the walls and ceiling were no different in colour, but the room itself seemed brighter. Ivan's dull-brown hair was less dusty looking, the strands rich and gleaming like polished wood. How had she never noticed the flecks of yellow in the green eyes that now clinically surveyed her?

"Well?" Viktoriya asked. Her usually husky breath had gained not only depth but volume.

Alla faced the woman. Her heart skipped a beat. The already lush shade of Viktoriya's simple thigh-length jacket, paired with equally plain trousers, was now a deeper blue. And she glowed—a faint shimmer like the haze off a summer pond.

Viktoriya twitched and fidgeted on the spot like an impatient child. "Aren't you going to try some magic?"

She stared down at her hands. "Like what?" All she remembered of her power were the dramatic flares of it getting out of control.

"How about *this*." Viktoriya clasped Alla's hand, linking their fingers and raising them before each other.

Warmth slipped into her body and slithered along her veins, bringing a flush to her skin. She knew this feeling, albeit faintly. *Sharing power*. The sensation continued to flood her body, tingling through every nerve. It slipped into places heat had rarely gone and sent a fresh blush across her cheeks.

Alla leant closer and pressed her lips against Viktoriya's.

Her beloved hesitated for one flutter of a heartbeat before returning the kiss. They had indulged themselves in similar activities, usually in brief moments stolen from whatever tasks an heir to the crown was meant to perform.

None of those times had ever felt this decadent. The sweep of Viktoriya's lips was slow and hot. It consumed her thoughts and captured her breath. Her heart thrummed its tattoo of desire through her body.

With one arm wrapped around Alla's waist, Viktoriya pulled them closer together.

Alla stiffened as something poked her belly. She crushed herself against Viktoriya in an attempt to ignore the interjection, but it was definitely coming from her beloved's trousers.

Withdrawing just a bit, her lips still lightly touching Alla's with every breath, Viktoriya held her gaze with a heavy-lidded one. "Ivan?" she said, her voice hoarse.

"Leaving immediately, your highness," the Ghost replied, already heading towards the door.

Viktoriya relinquished her hold on Alla's waist as soon as the door clicked shut. She stepped back, remaining hunched over. "I'm sorry. I don't usually—" She pressed a hand to her mouth, visibly gathering strength. "I am very attracted to you and we were already sharing energy, then we kissed and—" She hung her head. "I'll do better at controlling it."

Without thinking, Alla's gaze flicked down to the notable bulge in Viktoriya's trousers before returning to the woman's face. Or rather, the hand that shielded her features. "Are you all right?" It hadn't been its presence that had surprised her, as Viktoriya had explained how she had the relevant equipment to impregnate another with her child. Alla just hadn't expected it to react so eagerly. "Do you need me to leave for a bit?"

"Yes," Viktoriya mumbled. She lowered her hand before Alla could take more than a few steps towards the door. "I mean, I'll be fine. Stay. Please."

Alla stopped and remained silent as she waited for her beloved to regain a small measure of composure.

"God, I just—" Viktoriya exhaled in a trembling blast. "I'm fine. I will be. I *am*. I... This isn't the first time it—" She held up a hand towards Alla whilst covering her lips with her other fingers. "It's just been a while."

"Since you've had sex?"

That dark gaze finally met Alla's. Her eyes looked wider and deeper than before. She shook her head. "Since it's been... erect." The word seemed to reluctantly slither from her lips. "I didn't think how sharing magic would affect me. Or how pleasant a sensation it would be. I..." She wet her lips, trapping the bottom one between her teeth.

Since learning that Viktoriya wasn't a prince, she hadn't given much thought about the parts her beloved possessed. She had known for some time, but it seemed odd to put such weight on one part of a whole person. She would've loved her princess no matter what was in her trousers.

She struggled to think of how it would feel to possess a part of her body that seemed like it shouldn't be there, let alone what might run through the mind upon said part reacting in equally unwanted ways. "Have you ever been intimate?" The question was out before she could think. She had no personal experience herself, but it hadn't occurred to her that Viktoriya might be in the same boat.

Again, Viktoriya shook her head. A small huff of amusement escaped her nose. "Who with? Not that I haven't thought about it," she confessed, her gaze suddenly refusing to meet Alla's. "I know the theory behind sex. That is, I have been taught the usual methods. And some of the ways to pleasure someone both with and without penetration." One side of her mouth hitched up. "But—" She fell silent as Alla laid a finger on her lips.

"It's new for me, too."

A rough laugh barked out Viktoriya's mouth. "Oh, good. We can be awkward and inept together on our wedding night."

Which would be some months from now. "Maybe," she

whispered, her cheeks growing hot at the boldness of her thoughts. "We could try before then? Especially if you're uncomfortable with certain actions." If the idea had run through Viktoriya's mind as she claimed, then letting her darker thoughts stew would only see her reaction worsen. "We could take it slow and stop if you're finding it too much."

Gently laying her hands on Alla's hips, Viktoriya drew her close once more. "Just when I think my love for you couldn't possibly be any greater. But that isn't my concern. And there's something else I've wanted to show you that I couldn't until we removed the chain from your neck."

"Oh?" Alla thought she had travelled all over the palace since her arrival. She hadn't discovered anywhere barred to her beyond personal chambers. What little corner of her new home had she missed?

Viktoriya linked their fingers. The touch was warm, but lacking the earlier buzz of magic. "Come. We'll take the back way there. If anything, it'll give both of us time to cool ourselves. If I'm not mistaken, you're as warm as I." She pressed the back of her fingers against Alla's cheek. "You certainly feel it."

Alla closed her eyes. The allusion to her flustered state only added more heat to her burning face. "Lead the way. But Ivan's going to be so mad when he finds out you're not here." The man truly did have his work cut out in safeguarding the empire's future ruler.

The announcement gained her a whispering chuckle.

Hand in hand, they strolled through the halls. Alla thought they might descend to the treasury—it was another place she had been barred from—but their journey wove ever upwards towards the centre of the palace. She tried to keep track of the turns and side corridors they took, but became lost after the third flight of twisting stairs.

"Not far now," Viktoriya said as they slipped through a gap in the wall hidden behind a heavy bookcase.

The air in the corridor smelt of disuse and dust, although she saw no sign of the latter gracing the floor. Beyond a few high windows, the only opening was a door at the other end of the corridor, a single hulking thing made of pitted steel with a knob and keyhole in the middle.

Just looking at it set the hairs on Alla's neck to tingling. She halted a good few camel lengths from it. "What's on the other side?"

"Something far older than this empire." Viktoriya laid a hand on the door, the other clasping her necklace. "But before I show you..." She unbuttoned her jacket as Alla watched on in confusion. She started to do the same with her shirt, then stopped. "There's something I need to tell you about me."

Alla clasped Viktoriya's arm. The two layers of fine linen and silk sleeves did little to hide the tension in the muscles beneath. What could her beloved tell her that she didn't already know? If there was anything else, then they would work through it together. "I already know all about you."

"Not this." The small, slightly embarrassed smile returned to Viktoriya's lips. She undid her shirt and parted it in one quick tug of cloth, letting the fine fabric flap limply in the musty breeze creeping down the hall. "I am part elf." She took Alla's hand and placed it on her chest. "Here. See?"

Alla ran her hands along Viktoriya's skin. She slid further downwards as the air gusting from the woman's lips grew ragged. Muscles flexed and relaxed beneath Alla's fingers with every harsh breath. Was this the first time anyone had touched her this way? How starved she must've been. To crave even the smallest of brushes and have to shun it for fear of someone announcing her true self to the world before she was ready.

Hesitantly cupping the back of Alla's head, Viktoriya drew her close enough to press her lips to Alla's forehead as if the intoxicating kiss they had already shared in Alla's chambers hadn't happened. "Do you feel it?"

"No." Whilst the chest was quite smooth and hairless for a human—as well as absent of the usual curves and breasts of a woman—there was nothing to suggest Viktoriya was elven.

With her beloved guiding her touch, Alla slid her hands down Viktoriya's sides where her fingers were greeted by a curious anomaly.

She had assisted with enough injured serfs to know what a healthy human chest should feel like when it came to rib position. "Thirteen." Certainly not the right number. Not for a human. "You *are* part elven." That was the only possible conclusion.

Viktoriya regarded her from beneath her lowered lashes. "Yes." She brushed Alla's hair back from her ear. "Not as obvious as your tells." Her fingers continued to slide along the underside of the point.

Blissful warmth shimmied its way down Alla's body at the touch. It pooled in her gut, feeding that same desire sharing power had given her.

However much the sensation fogged her mind, it held no sway over her tongue. "I know there's elven blood in you from centuries back, but for there to still be signs..." Elven blood announced itself strongly in half-elves. Those superficial tells faded quickly without additional strengthening, often leaving hidden signs in the bones. "It would mean that it was—"

"Recent?" Viktoriya inclined her head. "Yes. My great grandmother, in fact."

She recalled the portrait readily enough. It hadn't seemed as altered as the others. Living within the palace walls, she had the means to become well acquainted with every single one. Each study only made her surer, but she couldn't believe she had missed one. "And how many of the others?" Not all of them or else Viktoriya wouldn't look this human. She'd be leaner, shorter. Her fingers longer. Her ears and canines more pointed.

"Every fourth or fifth queen."

"All the way down the line." It wasn't a question. There weren't any portraits of the rulers going back as far as the time of elven settlement. If she could find signs amongst some of the older portraits that *did* exist, there was no reason why it couldn't be there at the beginning.

Surprise lifted Viktoriya's brows. "Yes. Almost ever since the first elves arrived on the continent." She seemed to relax as they talked and was certainly less concerned with Alla's touch and proximity.

Alla removed her hand and allowed her beloved to redress. "Why?" Her stepmother hadn't been the only one to see elves as inferior. So many had entered Niholia as refugees, or worse, from the Udynea Empire. It had been over a millennium, but that knowledge was still strong.

Shrugging, Viktoriya fiddled with the key hanging around her neck. Even when she removed all other jewellery, that key remained. "Because of what they had."

Alla tried to think on what the elves of old could've possibly possessed that would be of any interest to the original royal line. "The orb?"

Viktoriya nodded. "You've noticed it, then."

How could she not? Every single painting had two things in common—the key and the swirling red and white orb.

Her gaze flicked to the door. That must be what waited on the other side. The reason her beloved had brought her here. "Can I see it?"

Viktoriya beamed. "I can do you one better." Twitching her brows, she removed the key from around her neck and unlocked the heavy metal door. There was a mischievous note to her voice, matching the impish spark lighting her eyes.

It sent a dreadfully wicked tingle through Alla's spine and warmed her to the core. She ran a hand along the neck of her overdress. The corridor was far too stifling for so many layers and she didn't think this particular heat would dissipate whilst strolling through the palace halls.

Alla expected the door to give an ominous groan as Viktoriya pushed it open, but the metal panel swung silently inward. Ponderous, but effortless.

The room was circular and dim, illuminated only by the light filtering through the corridor's windows and the soft ruddy glow of the marbled red and white orb. It sat upon a squat pillar, couched in dark velvet.

Elven. She'd never seen anything from that side of her heritage. Everyone believed all the elven artefacts were long gone, stolen or destroyed by the Udynea Empire. But here was one. It filled her vision and consumed her thoughts.

She stepped closer, her heart thundering in her ears.

The orb's glow changed as she crossed the threshold, blazing like an ember.

At her back, Viktoriya gave a satisfied grunt.

"What's happening?" Alla said over her shoulder, unable to tear her gaze from the orb. Her hand twitched. The desire to gather it to her had her taking another step.

"It's just reacting to your elven blood." Viktoriya joined her within the room. "This is where the strength of my family's power lies. It holds a special ability to gift those who touch it a glimpse of the future. All those of elven blood can potentially use it, but only through specific lines can it be controlled."

"Your bloodline." Not an unreasonable assumption. The orb wouldn't be given such a place of prestige if it was worthless to the royal line.

Viktoriya nodded as she stood beside the orb. "The ability gets diluted through the generations. Every so often, an elven child is chosen to become the next tsarina raised and prettied up." She bowed her head. "It would've been my grandchild's fate to have their wife chosen at birth, but the gods led me to you." Her gaze flicked up, dark and wanting. "To let love dictate for a few generations more. This world is broken and I intend to fix it. With you at my side, I will change the empire and bring Niholia forward into an enlightened age where people cannot be traded or sold."

"How?"

"Let's see." She slammed her hand down on the orb and stiffened. Her eyes glazed over, staring at nothing and at everything at the same time. It could've been a trick of the light, but they seemed to glow the same ruddy colour of the orb.

"Vik?" Alla took a hesitant step forward. What could she do? What should she do? Would breaking contact with the orb stop her from seeing— What was it? *Glimpses of the future.* Clearly bright ones judging by the wide smile. "What do you see?"

"I—" Pain flickered across her face. She sank to her knees, clearly dazed. Her fingers slipped from the orb. A twitch of her forefinger sent it tumbling off its velvet bed.

Alla lunged for it, catching the orb before it hit the floor.

Visions flashed before her, most too disjointed or blurred to understand. A ship in ruins, left stranded high above the waves. A land in chaos, terror swarming the forest whilst a great tree was brought to cinders and ash. Battles raged across lush fields, the green turning black as metal-covered caravans rumbled through the dead, belching smoke and spitting metal.

With great effort, she slipped the orb into her skirts. The visions stopped. What had already poured into her mind played on, but nothing new joined them. She laid a hand on Viktoriya's shoulder. The fabric beneath her fingers was damp with sweat. "Are you all right?" Had she seen the same images?

"Yes." The word came softly, low and slightly distant. With her breath rasping through her lips, she took Alla's hand and kissed the back of it. "I for one," she murmured, sounding less dazed, "Am definitely glad to have found you, my dear Alla."

Alla folded her legs beneath her and joined her beloved on the floor, making sure the orb remained nestled in her skirts. "Me too."

They remained there with their knees touching and their fingers linked until Viktoriya had caught her breath. The hum of magic circulated between them like water on a wheel, lazy and rhythmic. It was almost enough to lull Alla to sleep.

And it must have for, after what felt like only a short moment, she became aware of Viktoriya's warm breath on her forehead before her beloved's lips pressed to her temple.

"Rest a little longer, love," Viktoriya insisted as Alla went to stand. "It would seem holding the orb has taxed you even more than myself."

"I saw—" She fell silent at Viktoriya's gentle, albeit insistent, shushing.

"It doesn't matter what you saw. Not right now." Briefly unlinking their fingers, she ran a thumb across Alla's shoulder. "I will arrange for a scholar to teach you how to control your magic tomorrow. You've so much raw strength. Such talent needs tempering."

Alla lazily peered out from beneath one eyelid, her gaze sliding to the orb still resting in her lap. Giving a soft hum of agreement, she drifted off on the buzz of magic thrumming through her veins.

Epilogue

Alla impatiently shuffled from one bare foot to the other. The weight of her gown seemed to flow around her like a waterfall. Did she really need so much? All the pale blue fabric was far more than she had ever worn in her life, even with the past few months of living alongside Viktoriya. But it *was* her wedding dress.

She had spent the better part of a year in the palace, learning what was expected of her whilst preparations for the wedding continued all around. According to the high priest's divination, summer was the most auspicious time for a child to be conceived and thus perfect for the wedding.

Her wedding. On *this* day. In just a few hours. By the time the sun had set, she would be a princess. An unashamedly half-elven princess.

The tsar had been livid at the idea. Not of his daughter marrying Alla, but of her being so open about her heritage. She had been ready to agree in hiding her ears during the ceremony, but Viktoriya insisted otherwise.

Alla balled her hands in an effort to resist jigging on the spot like a lunatic. *Today.* She could barely contain her excitement. Or was it nerves? It seemed as though she felt everything at once.

Or was that a sign of life growing in her belly? They hadn't been intimate too many times—it would've been too unseemly for the princess to routinely sneak into Alla's chambers. But whilst she hadn't the common illness that afflicted most women, she was starting to get a little pudgy in all the right places.

She caught her reflection in the dressing mirror and dragged her fingers across her neck where the magic-suppressing chain had once hung. Even after all these months, the lack of the chain's weight felt strange.

The removal had drastically altered her perception of the world. Not only did the colours seem brighter and the sounds clearer, but everything was stronger. What had once been a powerful taste or smell now nearly incapacitated her. And her emotions seemed beyond control, especially when Viktoriya touched her. Even an innocent kiss stirred all sorts of feelings. At least her magic remained in her control.

Tempering her magic hadn't helped with the orb. She had hoped, but diverting the visions to what she wanted to see was beyond her abilities. It showed her the same thing, smoke and fire... and death.

Alla shuddered. She would *not* think of it. Not on this day.

"Hold still, my lady," Odette said as she fussed with Alla's skirts. "Just one final touch."

A flash of colour in the mirror caught Alla's eye. Mady fluttered from one side of the room to the other like an indecisive butterfly. The impression wasn't at all helped by her off-white dress with long, flowing sleeves. Whilst Mady had been seemingly content to sit quietly as Alla dressed, Alla's own impatience had apparently rubbed off on the girl, much like her stubbornness and curiosity, all to Odette's consternation.

After months busying herself with one palace task to another, Mady's interests had landed squarely on the ships that sailed into the palace's private docks. Her tendency to scurry aboard at every opportunity kept Odette on her toes. Already, Alla could see herself trying to convince one of the merchants to let the girl sail with them, even if it was only a short distance. It would have to be soon before the unthinkable happened and Alla lost her, just like she had done with almost everyone else.

Unbidden, her mind drifted back to her stepmother and stepsisters. She hadn't thought of them in months, but recent word from the Obuzan border had snapped them back into the forefront of her mind.

Her stepmother had been wrong about how well her daughters would fare on the northern border. Tamara had managed to survive fighting for a number of months before an ambush had left her without the use of her left side. Natalya was still out there. Although, no one could say for certain which side of the border she currently resided on.

Her stepmother, however, had fallen in her first battle.

Alla had seen to the woman's burial—within the grounds of the estate's graveyard, although far from her parents. Not that there had been much to bury. She was still family.

Like it often did when she thought of her stepmother and stepsisters, her thoughts drifted to the estate. It had been a month since she had stepped foot on the familiar land.

Even though Odette assured her things were running smoothly, Alla wished she could see it for herself. Since leaving to live in the palace, she tried to visit the mansion every other week, but the wedding preparations had usurped every scrap of spare time. It wasn't quite home anymore, but a part of her was drawn to the land. It was hers. Completely. No one could steal the place where her memories resided.

With her ownership verified by the crown, Alla had wasted no time in firing the whip-happy serf master, then freeing the serfs bought by her stepmother. She hired skilled servants to train those who were willing to stay or replace those who moved on.

Her efforts had seen both the people and the fields thrive.

During her visits, Alla often spent her time checking on the running of the farm, ensuring the people weren't abused, that the land continued to grow and, lately, that the modifications to the mansion were on schedule.

So much had changed over the months. Walking through the estate felt like a dream. People still toiled—the work required was no less taxing—but there was a different energy to it. Determination instead of indifference. Pride and joy instead of terror.

It was still awkward having them pay their respects as she passed—she had struggled alongside some for so many years. Often, her retinue of royal bodyguards had to hold her back from mucking in wherever an extra hand looked welcomed. She understood why her father used to spend most of his days out in the fields or her mother had assisted with the animals.

Her gaze slid to where her parents' portraits sat on either side of her dresser. How she wished either one had lived to see it. She knew her father well enough to know he would've approved. But her mother? She remembered so little.

"Do you think she would be proud of me? Of what I've done with the estate?"

Odette halted in her task of straightening the pleats in Alla's skirts. "Who?"

"My mother."

Brushing off her hands, Odette cradled Alla's head as if they were back in the mansion and she was a child newly stripped of her parents. "Your mother was a fierce woman, my lady. She'd a tongue that could cut lead and a heart big enough to fit the world. If she could see you now, she would burst with pride. Just like your father." Her unshed tears gleamed in the lantern light. "Just like me."

Swallowing in an attempt to relieve the tightness in her throat, Alla threw her arms around the woman's shoulders. "I miss them so much," she whispered, words she had barely been able to think let alone utter for so long.

The sharp tattoo of knuckles on the door snapped Alla back into the present. Was it time to depart for the temple? Was she ready? A quick glance in the mirror confirmed everything was in its proper place.

Except she still hadn't any shoes. She owned several now, even though she preferred to go barefoot. None of them seemed fitting for this cloud-like gown. *Vik said she had it in hand.* Perhaps that was one of the servants sending them over now. *Talk about last minute.*

Another loud rap on the door sent Odette scurrying to open it.

Viktoriya waited on the other side. She froze in the doorway, openly admiring Alla. "You look heavenly." She walked in, the train of her crystalline blue dress trailing behind her and so long that it only finished entering once her beloved had reached the centre of the room.

"And *you* shouldn't be here." They were supposed to meet before the temple doors. "Do you have Ivan chasing after you again?"

Viktoriya rolled her eyes and, sticking out her tongue, blew a low flatulent sound. "Of course not, he's right here." She waved a hand at the empty doorway before giving an exasperated huff. "Honestly, Ivan. We're all dressed. You *can* enter."

The Ghost guard marched into the room, clutching a small chest as though it was his only protection from the princess' ire. Not that Viktoriya ever chastised the man. If anything, it was the other way around after his charge had impulsively darted off on some adventure. "For you, my lady." Ivan offered the chest to Alla, indicating that she open it immediately with a dart of his eyes and a twitch of his brow.

Inside sat her stepsister's crystalline shoes. The ones she had left behind when they'd exited her family's mansion. She thought them lost. "I can't wear these. They don't fit me." She was certain to trip if she walked the temple aisle in them.

Viktoriya took up one of the shoes and knelt before Alla. "Try them, you'll be pleasantly surprised."

Alla hitched up her skirt and extended a leg.

The shoe glided onto her stocking-clad foot, sitting snugly as if made for her. "It fits? How?"

"Magic," Viktoriya purred before a deep chuckle shook her shoulders. "This is *my* wedding. My parents spared no expense. With all the artisans around, it wasn't hard to find someone with the knowhow to make an adjustment."

"But they're made of glass."

Viktoriya nodded. "The finest quality." She stood with a fluid grace. Alla couldn't imagine how she managed it whilst garbed in so much fabric. "Ready to take your place at my side?"

Alla nodded. All those years of being told where she belonged, of her every dream ground to dust...

Never would she have thought that finding that place could happen whilst stepping out in borrowed shoes.

"One last thing." Viktoriya pushed back the curls concealing Alla's ears. "No more pretending. We show the world precisely who we both are."

Alla nodded. She hadn't left her chambers with her ears on display before, but she could do this. "No more hiding." She raised her foot as Odette helped her don the other shoe, admiring the glint in the lantern light. This might not have been the path her parents had ever envisioned, but it was hers now. A destiny shaped through her own choosing, through being as she was meant to be. By remaining true to herself, she had found what her parents had wanted the most.

A place where she was safe. Where she could be herself.

And be loved.

THE END

About the Author

Aldrea Alien is an award-winning, bisexual New Zealand author of speculative fiction romance of varying heat levels.

She grew up on a small farm out the back blocks of a place known as Wainuiomata alongside a menagerie of animals, who are all convinced they're just as human as the next person (especially the cats). She spent a great deal of her childhood riding horses, whilst the rest of her time was consumed with reading every fantasy book she could get her hands on and concocting ideas about a little planet known as Thardrandia. This would prove to be the start of The Rogue King Saga as, come her twelfth year, she discovered there was a book inside her.

Aldrea now lives in Upper Hutt, on yet another small farm with a less hectic, but still egotistical, group of animals (cats will be cats). One thing she hasn't yet found is an off switch to give her an ounce of peace from the characters plaguing her mind, a list that grows bigger every year with all of them clamouring for her to tell their story first. It's a lot of people for one head.

aldreaalien.com

Printed in Great Britain
by Amazon

20822355R00078